CHRISTMAS ON Mill Street

A Novel by

JOSEPH WALKER

SHADOW MOUNTAIN

Visit us at ShadowMountain.com

Library of Congress Cataloging-in-Publication Data

Walker, Joseph, 1955–
   Christmas on Mill Street / Joseph Walker.
     p. cm.
   ISBN 978-1-59038-804-4 (hardbound : alk. paper)
   I. Title.
   PS3623.A35946C48 2009
   813'.6—dc22   2009011625

Printed in the United States of America
Publishers Printing, Salt Lake City, UT

10   9   8   7   6   5   4   3   2   1

Prologue

I should probably remember the Cuban Missile Crisis. I really should.

I mean, I was nine years old at the time. That's old enough to be relatively aware of what's going on in the world, isn't it? I've gotta believe the Cuban Missile Crisis was in all the papers. I'll bet Walter Cronkite even talked about it—probably a lot. And around our house, when Walter Cronkite said, "That's the way it is" . . . well, that's the way it was.

But it was October, 1962, and I was busy. Fourth grade was no piece of cake, especially the way Miss Greene pushed and prodded (she could be excused for this because she was young and beautiful as far as teachers go, and she was from Canada, which made her . . . sort of . . . you know . . . exotic. And to a young man just discovering how interesting "beautiful" and "exotic" could be, that meant a lot). Besides, the Yankees were struggling in the World Series against the Giants, and Mickey Mantle needed every ounce of concentrated support I could muster. Everyone was learning to do a dance called the Twist, and *almost* everyone recorded a song about it—everyone from Chubby Checker to Frank Sinatra. And there was this cute, dark-haired girl named Rhonda in my neighborhood, and . . . well, it was hard work to appear to be completely disinterested whenever I was around her—you know what I mean?

Still, I might have been vaguely aware of the fact that the United States and the Soviet Union were within an itchy trigger finger of turning the planet into subatomic particles, had it not been for Mill Street.

My family had just moved to Utah from Arizona, and I was still trying to fit in with the boys in the neighborhood. They were a great group of guys, and nobody was mean to me or anything. But they had all lived in the neighborhood all their lives, and they had known each other . . . well . . . forever (Jimmy and Johnny had known each other longer than forever, but that didn't really count, because they were twins). So as winter approached, I was still feeling like an outsider—a tall, overweight, semi-clumsy outsider.

Oh, and did I mention that I stuck out like a sore thumb because of my height and weight? I was sort of used to it. I was born big (10 pounds, 14 ounces and 23 inches long—Dad said that when I was sprawled out in the hospital nursery bassinette it looked like I had been held over from the last class), and I had always been big, so it wasn't exactly a new experience for me. But still, it didn't help me fit in with the crowd—you know?

Which is probably why I became so focused on Mill Street when the boys started talking about it.

"My dad says it's all about weight," said Jimmy, whose father was an engineer and should know about such things. "Weight and wax. Those're the keys."

"Nah," said Danny, shaking his head. "It's speed. You get enough speed going at the top, and it'll take you all the way."

"I don't know," Billy said. "I got going pretty fast last year, and I still couldn't make it past Bennetts'."

"You weren't going that fast," Danny said. "And you were dragging your feet before you got to the first bend."

"Was not!"

"Was too!"

"Was not!"

"Was—"

"What're you guys talking about?"

I had been present for the entire conversation, but I couldn't for the life of me figure out what they were saying. Sort of like that song I heard on the radio once in a while: "Besame, besame, besame mucho, besame, besame, besame, besame mucho . . ."

What the heck was that about?

"We're talking about Mill Street," Jimmy said patiently. "You know, over on the other side of the school? The big hill?"

"Ohhh," I said, nodding knowingly even though in my mind I was thinking: *There's a big hill on the other side of the school?*

"And we're talking about sledding all the way to the end—all the way to Orchard Drive," Johnny said. "Nobody's ever done it before."

"My brother Brent did it," Billy insisted.

"Brent isn't heavy enough," Jimmy said. "My dad said you have to be—"

"Your dad doesn't know what he's talking about," Danny argued. "It's speed! You just need—"

"Wax," Billy insisted. "Brent said he used lots of paraffin wax, and that did the trick."

By now I was completely confused.

"You ride sleds on wax?" I asked. "I thought it was . . . you know . . . snow. Don't you ride sleds on snow?"

My friends stopped their argument to look at me. Then they started to laugh.

Suddenly I felt very Arizonan.

After they stopped laughing, Jimmy tried to explain. "Yeah, you ride sleds on snow," he said, speaking slowly, choosing his words carefully, as though he were talking to an idiot—which, of course, he was. "But some people like to rub wax on their runners because they think it makes the sled go faster."

"It does," Billy said. "Brent said it definitely does."

"Wax is for sissies!" Danny said. "What matters is your start. If you get a good running start you'll go faster and farther. Everybody knows that."

"A running start is good," Jimmy allowed. "And a little wax can help. But if you also have some weight on the sled—"

"I'll bet I can do it."

The words popped out of my mouth before I could think them through. And now it was too late to call them back.

"You?" Billy asked. "Do you even have a sled?"

"Well, no . . . not yet . . ."

"Have you ever even ridden a sled?" Danny wanted to know.

"Um . . . well . . . no . . . not exactly . . ."

"You've never even seen snow before, have you?" Jimmy said knowingly.

"Well, I've seen pictures . . ."

The boys looked at each other and grinned.

"You better wait a couple of years before you try Mill Street," Jimmy said. The way he said it made it sound like something to be afraid of.

"Yeah," Danny chimed in, still chuckling. "At least wait until you actually get a sled."

The boys laughed again and went back to their discussion. I pretended to listen, but inside I was seething. Sure, I was from Arizona, but how hard could it be to ride a sled down a hill? I mean, you sit on it and you go. Gravity sort of takes care of the rest.

Especially if you have a substantial gravitational base— which, of course, I had. That was the part that spurred me on and gave me the courage to suggest that I could make the run down Mill Street, all the way to Orchard Drive (wherever the heck *that* was). Jimmy's dad had said that weight would make a difference. Well, I certainly had weight on my side. On my front and back, too—no question about that. So even if I didn't make it all the way to Orchard Drive, at least I could make it farther than my lightweight friends. I was sure of it.

The only thing I wasn't sure about was the sled. I didn't have one. But Christmas was coming . . .

Chapter One

I'm not sure why I decided to dress up as Fidel Castro for Halloween that year. Like I said before, I really had no idea what was going on ninety miles off the southern shores of Florida. Heck, I was only vaguely aware of Florida. So things like the Bay of Pigs and creeping Communism and all those missiles pointed at Washington, D.C., didn't really motivate me. Now, if those missiles had been pointed at Disneyland or someplace meaningful like that, it would have been another thing altogether.

In retrospect, the thing that probably prompted me to dress up as Castro for Halloween was the cigar. Fidel was either holding one or smoking one in every picture I had ever seen of him (which, come to think of it, was a grand total of two—maybe three). And since I had a foot-long plastic stogie left over from the previous year's hobo costume . . . well, the transition from homeless vagabond to totalitarian dictator seemed natural to me.

But not to Mom.

"You want to be *what*?"

After eight children, you'd think that Mom would have seen and heard pretty much everything. But I took pride in occasionally coming up with something that seemed to stump her—or to at least make her wonder why she didn't stop after seven children.

"Castro," I said. "You know—that beardy guy who wants to blow up Philadelphia?"

Having lived with me for nearly eight years, Mom had a pretty good bead on how my brain worked. So she understood immediately what I was trying to say.

"You mean Florida," she said. "Castro wants to blow up Florida, not Philadelphia."

"Yeah," I said. "Well, I knew it was one of those f-places."

I'm sure she was tempted to go into the whole "f," "ph," "gh" (as in "tough") thing, but she knew me well enough to know that once we started down that road we were doomed to follow it through to its illogical end, which meant we would probably never get around to answering her original question. So she let the spelling slide in favor of the costuming.

"Why do you want to be Castro for Halloween?"

Why? Well, there were a million reasons. The cigar. The beard. The army fatigues. The fact that he was on TV almost as often as Annette Funicello, every boy's favorite Mouseketeer (and—don't tell anyone, okay?—my first crush). A million reasons.

Only I couldn't think of any at the moment.

"I don't know," I said after a fairly pregnant pause.

"You don't know?" Mom asked, her dark eyes flashing and her carefully coiffed black hair bobbing. "You don't know who he is? You don't know what he stands for? You don't know what he almost did to our country last week?"

Mom was the disciplinarian in our family. Don't get me wrong—she was sweet and kind and loving, just like a mother is supposed to be. I adored her. But I also feared her. She wasn't a tall woman; she was just an inch or two taller than I was at the time, and I was only in the fourth grade, for Pete's sake. But she was stocky and tough, and she had a way of looking at you— hands on hips, head slightly bowed with her eyes glaring at you over the top of her glasses—that made you want to run and hide behind your mother.

Except . . . she *was* my mother.

"Well," I stammered, trying to come up with something . . . anything . . . "Um . . . he . . . you know . . . wants to blow up . . . um . . . Philadelphia . . . I mean . . ."

"He wants to blow up America!" she said emphatically. "He wants to wipe us off the face of the earth—him and that Khrushchev."

Khrushchev! I knew who *he* was. My big sister Linda told me about him a few nights earlier when I was hauling the trash out to the metal garbage can on the other side of the garage.

"Watch out for the Russians," she whispered as I pushed open the screen door leading out into our secluded, unlit backyard, our overflowing kitchen garbage pail in hand.

"What are Russians?" I whispered back.

"You know—Khrushchev," she replied with all the accumulated wisdom a fifteen-year-old can muster. "The guy on TV who looks like Grandpa Arrowsmith."

"You mean he's in our backyard?" I asked. He was such a mean-looking little guy, especially when he was mad and pounding his shoe on the table, that the thought of him being in our backyard really *was* scary.

"Well, probably not," Linda allowed. "But his soldiers might be out there."

"Why?" I asked.

"They like chubby blond boys," she said very seriously. "They brainwash 'em and train 'em for their armies."

I wasn't exactly sure what brainwashing was, but at that point in my life *any* kind of washing was intolerable. And since I was both chubby *and* blond, I figured I was a goner for sure. So I made Linda walk out to the trash can with me, which gave her time to point out some searchlights off in the distance, which she said were searching for Martians. Interestingly, she said that the Martians were here because they were also looking for chubby blond boys, even though she wouldn't say why because "it's just too horrible to talk about."

So, yeah, I knew all about Russians and Martians, and if

Castro was one of them . . . well, I understood why Mom was so upset.

Mom continued. "And they would have wiped us off the face of the Earth if President Kennedy hadn't figured out what they were up to and stood up to them." Suddenly, an idea occurred to Mom. "You could go as President Kennedy! That would be fun, wouldn't it?"

I thought about it for a second. President Kennedy was cool. I mean, he and his family played touch football on the White House lawn—how cool was that? We all tried to imitate his accent (you haven't lived until you've heard western boys try to do a New England accent: "We are now going to play, and we are going to do it with great vig-ah!"). Kennedy also had a cute daughter about my age (my second crush). And I kind of liked the idea of trick-or-treating with a new mantra: "Ask not what trick I can do for you; ask what treat you can give to your neighb-ah!"

But President Kennedy had really cool hair and was thin and handsome. I had a butch cut and was pudgy and . . . well . . . I figured I could do Castro, but I couldn't do Kennedy.

So I was the devil that Halloween. Mom was okay with that (don't ask me why it was not okay for me to be Fidel Castro but it was okay for me to be Satan. There are some things that defy theology and logic—especially on Halloween).

I went trick-or-treating with my new friends in my new neighborhood, and I've got to tell you, it was an eye-opening experience. You can tell a lot about your neighbors by the kind of treats they give out on Halloween. For example, I had already decided that my next-door neighbors, the Spencers, were cool. But I had no idea how cool they were until we went trick-or-treating at their house and they gave us mini-Hershey bars, the Holy Grail of Halloween candy. On the other hand, the Jensens—widely reputed to be the wealthiest family in the neighborhood—gave out apples. Apples! *Definitely* uncool. The only thing worse came from old lady Morris, who gave out pennies. I mean, she was just begging to have her yard toilet-papered.

Which, come to think of it, it was. Several times, as I recall.

I was using a pillowcase for my trick-or-treat bag, and it was getting pretty full despite all the candy I kept popping into my mouth as we laughingly, jokingly worked our way around the neighborhood. I was munching on a caramel popcorn ball when it suddenly occurred to me that we were in an area with which I was unfamiliar. It was dark, and there were only a few houses with lights on, so I couldn't really see where we were going. But it seemed somehow foreboding, with huge oak trees stretching their leafless fingers into the night sky, creating gnarled, menacing silhouettes against the Halloween moon. It didn't help that my friends were suddenly more quiet and sedate or that my heart was suddenly pounding—as much from the strange, unfamiliar, sort-of-spooky setting as from the fact that we seemed to be walking almost straight uphill.

"Hey, guys," I panted. "Where are we?"

"Mill Street."

I'm not exactly sure who said it. It might have been all of

them together in a sort of high-pitched, fourth-grade version of a Greek chorus. All I know is when they said it, my blood ran cold. Or at the very least, lukewarm.

Still, I tried to act . . . you know . . . nonchalant—which is pretty good, considering that at that point in my life I don't think I had even heard the word *nonchalant.* I stopped and turned around, peering through the darkness to try to make out the contours of Mill Street's much ballyhooed incline.

"So this is Mill Street," I said, pausing for effect. "It doesn't look all that steep."

That was an outright lie. At night, with only a few house lights breaking up the shadowy stillness, Mill Street looked more like a cliff than a street. Which is probably why the boys laughed derisively at my less-than-reverential assessment of their sledding Mecca.

"That's because it's dark, stupid!" Danny said. "Wait'll you see it in the daytime. Then you'll know what steep is."

I paused for a moment. I was actually trying to catch my breath from the uphill climb, but I acted as though I were surveying the night-shrouded landscape around me.

"So . . . where's Orchard Drive?" I asked, hoping to catch a glimpse of the point at which I would finally be basking in snow-covered glory.

"You can't see it from here," Johnny explained. "Mill Street bends right at the bottom of the steepest slope, then it bends left down there about two-thirds of the way to Orchard Drive.

That's why you have to do it on a sled, not a tube. You have to be able to turn. Twice."

"That's the tricky part," Jimmy said. "You have to be going fast enough that you can make it all the way to Orchard Drive, but if you're going too fast, you'll never make the turns."

"You should have seen Brian Stevenson last winter," Danny said, as Jimmy and Johnny both reacted to the memory. "He was going so fast at the second bend that he shot right off of Mill Street and into the Kimball's pyracantha bushes!"

"Yeah," Jimmy laughed, "he was picking berries out of his nose for a week!"

I wasn't exactly sure what a pyracantha bush was, but I figured they were something like the green bushes with thorns and reddish-orangish berries that were growing around our house.

"That's good to know," I said. "I'll have to be careful with that."

"Hey, you aren't still thinking about sledding Mill Street this winter, are you?" Danny asked.

"Sure," I said. "Why not?"

"Well, for one thing, you don't have a sled," Jimmy said.

"I'm getting one."

"Oh, yeah?" Jimmy asked. "What kind?"

There were different kinds? Who knew?

"Um . . . you know . . . the, uh . . . the good kind," I stammered.

"You're getting a Flexible Flyer?" Jimmy asked, clearly impressed.

"Yep," I said with so much feigned confidence Jimmy probably couldn't tell I was actually wondering what on earth a Flexible Flyer was and how I could convince either Santa Claus or my parents to get me one for Christmas.

"Well, a Flexible Flyer will help," Johnny allowed. "But you've gotta know how to ride it. *That's* gonna take some time."

"You need to start slow," Danny added. "Ride some of the little hills behind the school this winter. Then maybe next winter you'll be ready to try Mill Street."

"I'm going to ride it on Christmas Day," I announced as I turned to finish my first official ascent of Mill Street in the dark that Halloween night. "You'll see."

"Yeah, we'll see, all right," Danny said to Jimmy—quietly, and yet loud enough that I could overhear it. "We'll see his brains spread all over the Kimball's pyracantha bushes!"

A little ghoulish, perhaps. But, hey—it was Halloween.

The next day after school, I hopped on my bike, Ol' Blue. Blue was a little different from the bikes most of my friends had. They had those slick Schwinn Racers, with thin tires and three gears that helped them fly up hills with ease. Blue was a seven-year-old Murray that was actually my big brother Max's old newspaper delivery bike. Dad and Max had fixed it up, painted it a shiny shade of blue, and given it to me for Christmas the previous year, and I loved it. So what if it was big and klutzy and had oversize balloon tires? I was sort of big and klutzy too, and the balloon tires gave it a great ride—except for the time I tried to ride over a big rock in the road and was unceremoniously bounced off on my backside. That was on Christmas Day 1961, my first time riding Ol' Blue. I'd learned a lot since then.

And today I really needed to learn about Mill Street. I had to get a good look at it in the daylight so I would know firsthand what I was up against. I hopped on Blue and pedaled north, retracing our trick-or-treating route from the previous evening as nearly as I could remember. We were a good team, Blue and I. In my mind we were just like Tonto and his trusty pinto, Scout, tracking the bad guys for the Lone Ranger. And we must have been pretty good at it too, because faster than you can say "Kemosabe," we pulled up below a street sign etched in macabre black and stark white: "Mill Street."

"This doesn't look all that bad in the sunlight," I told Blue, who thankfully did not reply—this time. Indeed, the street's slope was relatively gentle at this point. To my left I could see where it ended less than a block away as cars moved briskly up and down a relatively busy street that I assumed was Orchard Drive. To my right, I could see the second of the two infamous Mill Street bends—but not the top of the street.

"I don't know what everyone was freaking out about last night," I told Blue as I pointed him east and started pedaling uphill. "This is easy! I could do this blindfolded!"

Almost immediately I noticed that it was getting harder and harder to pump Ol' Blue up the hill. The incline was getting steeper, yard by gut-wrenching yard, and the roadway seemed to be growing more narrow and less inviting. By the time I got to the first bend in the road, I was standing on the pedals, throwing my full—and considerable—weight into each pedaling pump.

Slowly I rounded the bend and looked up. Upper Mill Street loomed in front of me like a shrub-and-sidewalk-lined asphalt wall. The incline of the slope increased until it was almost vertical—at least, that's how it looked to me—and then it bent the other direction and continued to go up. And up. And up. Now, this may have been only my imagination, but I was pretty sure I could hear guys in lederhosen yodeling where the street bent at the base of the steepest incline. Then there were some Sherpas above that, and higher up, angels flapping their wings on top.

I got off Blue and started pushing him up Mill Street. My heart was pounding, as much from fear as from exertion. With every step my knees grew weaker and wobblier—literally and figuratively.

"This really *is* steep," I told Blue. I'm sure he would have agreed with me, but he was too busy gasping for air in his big balloon tires. "At least it will be fun riding back down."

Halfway up Mill Street's steepest stretch, I stopped to catch my breath and turned around and looked down. The sight made my knees feel weak, and I started wondering if there was any way to graciously back out of the boast to my friends. Maybe I could get polio—that would give me a good excuse, wouldn't it? Unfortunately, Mom had been pretty meticulous about making sure I was properly vaccinated, so that didn't seem likely. But what if I broke something? Not an arm—they'd still expect me to ride with a broken arm. But what about a leg? Or my back? That would work. A broken back would get me out of this for sure!

I reached the top of Mill Street and looked down. Way, way down. A broken back was a distinct possibility if I tried to ride Ol' Blue down this thing. Or a broken neck. Or—worse—a broken Blue. Thankfully I could see the school from where I stood, so I knew that there was another way home—along the top of the hill, in front of a couple of houses, over to the school and then down the familiar roads I walked every day to and from school. I took one last look at Mill Street and tried to imagine myself riding safely down its steep, snow-packed slope, successfully navigating both bends all the way to Orchard Drive.

I couldn't see it. Instead I could see . . . nothing special. Just a chubby kid standing alone at the top of a long, steep hill, willing to do anything to win the respect of the kids in his new neighborhood.

Well, *almost* anything.

I hopped on Ol' Blue and started riding slowly around the back way. Maybe it wouldn't snow. That was my only hope: if it never snowed in Utah again.

I wondered if it was wrong to pray for drought.

Chapter Two

Thunk! Thunk! Thunk!

By now the sound was unmistakable. I knew it by heart. It
sounded a lot like a hammer pounding on a melon. Only instead
of a melon, it was my head, which was being clobbered by Bette
Davis, who was laughing hysterically behind me as she thunk,
thunk, thunked away.

I had been having this same nightmare in black-and-white
pretty much every night since we saw *Whatever Happened to
Baby Jane?* at the Queen Theatre, so I was used to it. The thing
that shook me up this time was instead of my head cracking like
that doll's head on the *Baby Jane* posters, it popped right off my
neck and started bouncing down Mill Street, gruesomely thunking off of cars and trees and finally coming to a thorny stop in

Kimball's pyracantha bushes. And instead of Bette Davis cackling in the darkness, I looked up Mill Street to see Clara Morgan.

Clara Morgan lived right at the top of Mill Street, and she actually looked a little like Bette Davis. She was thin and frail, with wide-set, lashless eyes and a white, sickly pallor. I'm pretty sure she was even the same age as the famous actress. Of course, I may be way off on this. You know how it is with nine-year-old boys—everyone over twenty is the same age: *old*.

I had seen old lady Morgan only once before, when I caught a glimpse of her from the backseat of our Impala while she was standing in her dimly lit doorway as Mom delivered a loaf of freshly baked bread. Mostly I knew about her because our church congregation prayed for her nearly every week. My friends said they thought she couldn't come to church because she was a witch. My mom visited her once or twice every month, and she said Clara was sick with . . . well, I don't remember what it was, exactly, but it was awful. Whether she was a witch or an invalid, she was mysterious and unknown, which made her scary enough to replace Bette Davis in my nightmares—especially when my thoroughly thunked head was bouncing down Mill Street.

The first time I got a close-up look at Clara was the Sunday before Thanksgiving. She had asked to speak to the church congregation, and she approached the pulpit feebly, gripping it with all the strength her frail body could muster. Her voice was sweetly weak as she thanked two or three people who had done kind things for her during her illness. And then suddenly it turned sharp as she proceeded to chastise everyone else, from the lay leader of our congregation "who hasn't been to see me in months" to the "vicious little boys who steal my strawberries."

I looked at my friends, who were cringing guiltily behind their mothers and fathers.

"A price will be paid by this congregation for your neglect," she bellowed across the chapel. "A price will be paid! And you will have no one to blame for it but yourselves! Do you hear me? You have brought this on yourselves!"

With that, she turned with surprising vigor from the pulpit and stomped back to her seat in the congregation.

"See what I mean?" Jimmy said as we passed in the hall after the meeting was over. "She's a witch, and she just put a curse on us. We're all gonna wake up with snakes dangling from our ceilings."

Oh, great. Another nightmare. Just what I needed.

Still, I wasn't completely sold on the whole "witch" idea. I mean, Clara was scary and everything—that was for sure. But a really, truly witch? I didn't know about that. I was still trying to decide what I believed about all kinds of things, from Santa Claus to the Easter Bunny to Francis the Talking Mule. So I was anxious to see what my family would have to say about Clara around the Sunday dinner table.

At our house, Sunday dinner was the biggest and best meal of the entire week. Don't get me wrong—Mom cooked fine meals every day. My waistline was ample testimony to that. But on Sunday she pulled out all the stops, using every trick in her considerable culinary repertoire. A fried chicken dinner wasn't *just* fried chicken. It was homemade mashed potatoes and creamy chicken gravy. It was boiled, fresh green beans with onion and fried bacon. It was green Jell-O with pears and whipped topping. It was black and green olives and celery with cheese spread and Mom's special, homemade mustard pickles. And it was white cake with chocolate frosting for dessert. Every Sunday, Mom was Michelangelo, and Sunday dinner was her *David*. Only she created her *David* every Sunday for more than forty years.

Dad never helped much in the kitchen—that was Mom's domain, and only her daughters were allowed to help. But he made other contributions that helped make Sunday dinner a unique time for our family. Dad was a great communicator, red-headed and tall, handsome and personable—a people person. It was said of Dad that he could tell people to go to the hot, fiery, infernal regions below in such a way that they would actually look forward to the trip. And Sunday dinner was his chance to communicate with the people he loved most: us. Sunday dinner was a time to eat great food and to talk, and to savor and appreciate both. We talked about the world. We talked about our family—especially any particular problems any of us were having. We talked about Mom's delicious food. And we talked about church. It was part *Art Linkletter's House Party* and part Algonquin Round Table.

Only tastier.

As you might expect, Old Lady Morgan's tirade was the primary topic of discussion around the dinner table that Sunday. Dad was outraged over her inappropriate use of the Sunday service to grind her personal ax. Mom was hurt because she had actually made a significant effort to befriend Clara and wasn't mentioned among those who had been kind to her. Linda thought it was "dumb." Ann thought it was "scary." And I thought it was just one step closer to Clara thunking my head and sending it bouncing down Mill Street.

"It almost makes me wish I hadn't invited her over for Thanksgiving dinner," Mom said.

"What?" Dad blustered. "You invited that . . . that . . ."

"Witch?" I offered.

" . . . that woman to have Thanksgiving dinner with us?"

"Well, yes, Bud," Mom said. "What was I supposed to do? Her boys are all out of state. She doesn't have anyone else to have Thanksgiving with."

"But why does it have to be with us?" Ann whined. "She's scary!"

"She isn't scary," Mom said, albeit unconvincingly. "Clara is a sweet, decent person who has had a difficult and painful life—especially recently. She's just been hurt by a few things, and she had no other way to vent her frustration."

"Well, I don't care how frustrated she is," Dad said. "She had no right to do what she did in church today. No right at all."

"Look how clean my fork is!" Ann squealed. "Don't you just love how pretty and shiny it is? Pretty, pretty! Shiny, shiny!"

23

Uh, did I mention that my sister Ann is blonde? So "scary" only lasts so long with her—you know?

"Yes, dear, that's nice," Mom said. Then to Dad: "I agree that Clara was out of line today. But that doesn't change our Christian obligation to her as our neighbor."

"Technically, she isn't our neighbor," Linda said. "Technically, she's the Millers' neighbor, so they should have her over."

Mom corrected her. "Technically, we are *all* each other's neighbors—that's what Jesus taught. And the Millers have done plenty for Clara. It's our turn."

Dad found it difficult to disagree with Mom and impossible to disagree with both Mom and Jesus. So Thanksgiving dinner with Clara was on.

Shopping for Thanksgiving dinner was always a family affair with us. Linda and Ann would patrol the Safeway supermarket with Mom, ostensibly to help her but mostly to learn from her lifetime of accumulated wisdom and experience in the field of food.

"I usually prefer fresh green beans," she would say as they strolled up and down the store's wide, well-lit aisles, "but for the green bean casserole that we like to have with Thanksgiving dinner, the canned green beans work best. French-cut."

I don't know if my sisters really cared about what Mom was saying, but they nodded as if they were taking notes from Albert Einstein on the Unified Field Theory. And something must have stayed with them, because years later I could call either one of them for one of Mom's recipes and they would know it right off the top of their heads. It's kind of spooky, when you stop to think about it.

While Mom and my sisters were conducting a gastronomic colloquium in Safeway, I was next door in Skaggs, a drugstore that had all the stuff a boy could want: candy, toys, sporting goods, and . . . you know . . . stuff—not necessarily in that order. Mom had given me a nickel for a Baby Ruth candy bar, and I was wandering through the toy department and into the sporting goods, chomping on that wondrous mix of peanuts, caramel, chocolate, and nougat when I saw it gleaming—almost glowing—on the display rack in front of me: a shiny, brand-new sled.

"THE MOST THRILLING WORDS IN ENGLISH," the banner over the sled proclaimed: "FLEXIBLE FLYER."

It was difficult to argue with the "thrilling" part. My heart started pounding the second I saw the sled, with its sleek birchwood panels lacquered to a magnificent gloss, its bright red metal runners and struts, and its striking red-eagle trademark painted on the riding surface. It also had a wooden handle across the top—I figured that was to hold onto while you were flying downhill. At least, that was what the cartoon boy was doing in the drawing behind the sled—he was flying down a snowy hill. You could tell he was flying because there were straight lines in the drawing extending backward from his feet and from the sled itself. As a veteran cartoon and comic book reader, I understood that these lines meant that whatever was in front of them was moving fast. Really, really, way, way fast. And moving really, really, way, way fast is just what you would do on that sled—no question about it. The only question in my mind was did I want to move really, really, way, way fast down Mill Street?

I wasn't sure. The thought of lying down flat on that Flexible Flyer sled and somehow making my way around the Mill Street bends (what, no steering wheel?) and all the way to Orchard Drive was still overwhelmingly frightening to me. But I was sure about one thing: I wanted that sled. Not only was it the finest-looking piece of wood and metal I had ever seen, but I was also confident that owning it would substantially increase my standing among my friends in the neighborhood. They would think it was cool and, as a result, they would think I was cool. I would, of course, generously offer to let them take turns riding it, and they would have so much fun riding it themselves they would forget all about *me* riding it down Mill Street.

Maybe.

"Hey, doofus, it's time to go."

Ann had a way of making "doofus" sound like an insult.

"Look at this sled!" I told her. "Isn't that about the coolest sled you ever saw?"

Ann glanced at the Flexible Flyer casually and rolled her eyes.

"Mom wants you to come now," she said sternly.

"But it's a Flexible Flyer, and it can go really, really, way, way fast. Did you see the lines behind the boy's feet? That means—"

"It's fast. Yeah—I know. Look, Mom is heading for the car, and she's gonna be mad if you don't come right now."

"But I really want this sled for Christmas," I said as Ann turned and started walking away from me toward the front of the store. "Do you think I should bring her in here and show her? Is it too early to tell her what I want for Christmas?"

Ann paused, turned, and walked back to where I was standing, grinning all the way.

"I have an idea," she said. "Why don't you just tell Santa? Don't tell Mom or Dad. Don't tell Ellen or Julie or Mike or Mark or Max or Linda. Just tell Santa. If there really *is* a Santa, then it'll be okay—right?"

For several months Ann had been trying to convince me that Santa was a myth. This wasn't a new concept to me. I had been aware of the whole existence controversy for a couple of years, but I hadn't yet seen anything to convince me that Santa wasn't real. Still, Ann kept trying, providing circumstantial and anecdotal evidence that—okay, I'll be honest—occasionally troubled me. A little. I argued the point with her, but my arguments were becoming less strident. I needed something big, something compelling, something irrefutable that would prove Santa's existence once and for all—to Ann and to me.

And this might just be it.

"Okay," I said. "I won't tell anyone except Santa that I want a Flexible Flyer sled for Christmas. But if I get it, you have to tell everyone that I was right and you were wrong."

"It's a deal," Ann said, still grinning.

"And you have to take my turn drying the dishes for a month," I added.

Ann's grin broadened. "Let's make it two," she said. "Only it goes the same way for you. If you *don't* get a sled, you have to take my turn."

I hesitated, but only for a moment. The way I saw it, I had nothing to lose. If I did get the sled, Ann would be humiliated, and I wouldn't be drying dishes until March. Of course, I'd have to face Mill Street on my new sled, but what's a little pyracanthanization compared to the possibility of sibling mortification? And if I didn't get the sled, I'd have the perfect excuse to stay in and not face my friends—or Mill Street—at least until March.

The deal was done, but we didn't shake on it. That would require . . . you know . . . touching, and Ann and I usually tried to avoid that at all costs.

Thanksgiving morning was a whirlwind of activity, with everyone doing their part to help prepare for the feast—whether they wanted to or not. Mom was elbow-deep in the turkey—literally—doing unspeakable things to the poor dead bird. Whatever it was she was doing, I knew it was going to make the turkey and the stuffing taste extraordinarily good. Linda was peeling enough potatoes to feed an Irish army regiment, and Ann was preparing a relish tray with black and green olives, sweet and dill pickles, carrot and celery sticks, and, of course, cranberry sauce. The sights and sounds and aromas—oh, the rich, heavenly aromas—were enough to make you ravenously hungry long before the appointed hour for eating arrived.

In the rush of things, I had pretty much forgotten that we

were having a guest for dinner until Dad asked me to go with him to pick up Clara Morgan.

"Do I have to?" I whined, as only a fourth grader can.

"Yes, you have to," Dad said firmly. "It wouldn't be appropriate for me to pick her up alone, and everyone else here is busy."

"But she scares me," I complained, hoping honesty would overcome propriety.

Dad glanced at Mom, who was totally focused on the oven, where she was giving our turkey one last basting. "To tell you the truth," he said confidentially, "she scares me, too. So we might as well go and be scared together."

We didn't talk much as we drove through the neighborhood to the Morgan home. Dad was singing along with Perry Como on the radio.

Catch a falling star and put it in your pocket,
Never let it fade away.
Catch a falling star and put it in your pocket,
Save it for a rainy day . . .

Meanwhile, I was trying to figure out why Mill Street seemed so much less imposing when you were driving up it in a car instead of walking.

"My friends say this is a good sledding hill," I said as we motored slowly up Mill Street.

"It looks like a dangerous hill to me," Dad said. "Too many cars. You should sled on the hill behind the school."

"Well," I said, recognizing that I had to be very careful about what I was about to say, given the iron-clad nature of my agreement with Ann, "it will be tough to sled anywhere since I don't actually have a sled."

"I have an old one you can use," he said as we pulled into the Morgan driveway.

"You do?" This was definitely not good news. If Dad had an old sled for me to use, you could be relatively certain of three things: it would be woefully out of date, it wouldn't work well enough to be particularly useful, but it wouldn't be in such horrible shape that Dad would consider replacing it with a new one.

Oh, and one other thing: it for sure wouldn't be a Flexible Flyer.

No, this wasn't good news at all.

"I'll show you after dinner," he said as he slid out of the Impala. "You'll love it!"

I was pretty sure I wouldn't—but I didn't say that to Dad. Instead I sat in the car quietly as he walked up the front steps to pick up Mrs. Morgan. I was a little surprised when she came to the door smiling brightly and wearing a cheery red dress. I guess I was expecting a dour green complexion, a black dress, and a tall, pointy hat. But she greeted me kindly as Dad helped her into the car, and she was downright pleasant as we drove down the hill and through the neighborhood to our house. This was not at all what I was expecting, and it sort of threw me off a little. Then it occurred to me: she was probably just softening me up before she thunked my head off and sent it bouncing down Mill Street.

How devious. How macabre. How deliciously diabolical.

Suddenly I had new respect for her, even though I still couldn't bring myself to look her directly in the eye.

All thoughts of Mill Street mayhem vanished, however, as we walked from the car to the house.

"Oh, my!" Mrs. Morgan exclaimed as Dad helped her up the front steps and through our front door. "That smells so wonderful, it's making my mouth water!"

I didn't want to think about Clara Morgan drooling all over my house. Instead I focused on the miscellaneous aromas of roasted turkey, rich gravy, sage stuffing, and homemade rolls, providing sensory evidence to anyone within thirty feet of our house that an artist was at work therein.

And really, there was no question about it: Mom had The Gift—and not just at Thanksgiving. She could take Spam and do things with it that made you wish there really were such a thing as a Spam animal—and that you had been born one. She could turn a pot of beans and a few hot dogs into a dish so extraordinary you thought perhaps you would order beanie-weenies next time you dined at Chasen's. And her liver and onions . . . trust me. Heaven.

But Thanksgiving provided Mom with the perfect canvas for the full palette of her culinary colors. The turkey was hand-basted and stuffed with made-from-scratch dressing. The potatoes were properly mashed and covered with her rich, stewed chicken gravy. The yams were brown-sugar glazed and covered with enough gooey melted marshmallows to almost make them palatable to a confirmed non-yammer like me. Then there were the homemade rolls, homemade raspberry jam, mustard pickles, and pumpkin, banana cream, and coconut cream pies. It was always incredible—and incredibly good—and it appeared that Thanksgiving 1962 would be no exception.

Of course, Dad also had a special gift that came into play that Thanksgiving. Dad's gift was less appetizing, but it was every bit as much a part of our Thanksgiving tradition as Mom's green bean casserole. You see, Dad was a praying man. And not your common, ordinary, "Now I lay me down to sleep" sort of a praying man. When Dad prayed, angels stopped whatever they were doing to take notes. In my lifetime, I've heard Dad pray lost dogs home, failed businesses back into solvency, and prodigal children back into the fold. He was to praying what Willie Mays was to hitting a baseball. If there wasn't a God in heaven when Dad started praying, you just knew there'd be one by the time he said "amen."

Beyond being faithful, Dad was an articulate man who had a way with a phrase. So when Thanksgiving rolled around and it was time to give thanks for Mom's latest gastronomical triumph, no one was better suited to the task than my father. His prayers were always ponderous and profound, but on Thanksgiving they became epic—"The Lord's Prayer" meets *War and Peace*.

What can I say? He had The Gift.

Generally Mom and Dad's gifts blended remarkably well each Thanksgiving. Dad made sure to be properly thankful for "the loving hands which have prepared this magnificent repast," and Mom made sure to keep things warm on the stove until God had been properly thanked for all the work that Mom had done.

But on this particular Thanksgiving, Dad was too thankful for his own good. Maybe it was the presence of a special guest at our table. Maybe it was the family's still-relatively-recent move to a new state, or our country's recent brush with nuclear holocaust. Perhaps it was the shocking passing of Marilyn Monroe, the defeat of former Vice President Nixon in his California gubernatorial campaign, or the Supreme Court's recent decision to ban prayer in public schools. For whatever reason, Dad's pleas for mercy and guidance and his litany of thanks and blessing continued for nearly fifteen minutes (yes, I was timing him).

He was just blessing Congress, the president's cabinet, and the entire United Nations, when a new and unpleasantly pungent odor filled the room. None of us dared open our eyes, but we heard the distinct sound of Mom dashing for the kitchen and noisily slamming pots and pans long before any of us had a chance to say amen.

When at last we looked up and began trying to work out the kinks from our too-long-bowed necks, Mom was standing in the kitchen doorway with a blackened pan of burned, stewed chicken gravy.

"Perhaps you could pray a blessing of healing on our gravy," she suggested, fixing Dad with the icy stare of an artist whose finest creation had been sullied.

"There's nothing wrong with that gravy," Dad insisted. "It's just the way I like it!"

"Then I hope you'll enjoy every bite," Mom said as she ceremoniously placed the smelly pot before him. "The rest of us will be going without gravy this year, so it's all yours."

The rest of the dinner proceeded uneventfully, although there was a bit of understandable tension in the air. Clara did a commendable job of pointing out—several times, as I recall—that the mashed potatoes were so fluffy and delicious all by themselves that they didn't actually need gravy. I was so busy eating drumsticks and arranging my yams to make it look as though I had actually eaten some that I didn't really notice the absence of chicken gravy.

But Mom noticed it. And evidently it was discussed, because the next year, our Thanksgiving prayer was much shorter. Dad made sure of that by asking me to say it.

Even though I didn't have The Gift.

After dinner Dad and I took Clara home, and then Dad disappeared for a while. I assumed that he was hiding from Mom. At least, that's what I would have done. But then he poked his head in the back door.

"Sam!" he called brightly. "Come out to the backyard for a minute!"

"Ah, Dad," I whined from the basement where I was watching TV, "it's *Anything Can Happen Day!*"

Everybody knew that you just didn't miss *Anything Can Happen Day* on *The Mickey Mouse Club* because . . . well . . . anything could happen!

Everybody knew, that is, except Dad.

"Turn that TV off and get up here—NOW!" he said, forcefully enough that I snapped off the TV and headed upstairs, hoping with all my heart and soul that whatever I was missing on our black-and-white Motorola didn't involve Annette.

I stepped out of the back door and saw Dad standing in the yard holding a pile of wood. At least, that's what it looked like at first glance: dried-up old wood, with some rusty metal underneath.

"Are we stacking firewood again?" I asked, remembering not-so-fondly the ordeal of the previous week when we went into the mountains to gather some timbers for our fireplace and ended up bringing home dead wood that was infested with red ants, most of which seemed to like chubby blond boys as much as the Russians and Martians did.

"This isn't firewood," Dad said, a little hurt by my inability to see what he had in his arms. "This is Mike's old sled!"

My eldest brother, Mike, was fifteen years older than me, and I'm sure the sled Dad was holding—if that is indeed what it was—was old even when Mike was my age. From the looks of things, it was probably old when Dad was my age, and that was sometime around the Pilgrims or the pioneers (I always got those two confused). The wood was weathered white, with huge cracks and gaps where neatly polished slats should have been. The runners were completely rusted—in fact, the back end of the right runner had rusted clear off. And that cross-wise handlebar stick in the middle . . . well, there wasn't one. It was gone—just like my hopes of earning the respect and admiration of my new friends when I showed up with a shiny new Flexible Flyer for Christmas.

"Are you sure it will work?" I asked, wriggling a piece of wood that was just begging to be used as kindling.

"Of course it will work," Dad said. "And as I recall, this is a pretty fast sled. Mike used to really get going on this thing."

If I knew my big brother, that was probably because he had hitched it to the back of a car or a train or an airplane or something. Mike was our family James Dean—only without Natalie Wood—and I idolized him. And I had a hard time imagining him gently sliding down hills on a beat-up old sled.

"It looks like it could use some work," I said without much enthusiasm.

"A little," Dad allowed. "We'll sand it down, maybe put a little varnish on it. Then we'll wax up the runners, and it'll be good as new. You'll see."

What I could see was that Dad fully believed that this would be an adequate sled for me during my first winter in Utah. That was clear. It was equally clear that if I was going to get a brand-new Flexible Flyer sled for Christmas and avoid doing Ann's dishes for two months—two months!—it was going to be totally, completely up to Santa.

Whether or not he actually existed.

Chapter Three

You may call it a coincidence, but in my mind I was sure it was a Christmas miracle—even though it happened the day after Thanksgiving.

I mean, here I was in desperate need of Santa's intervention, up to my eyeballs in wonder, worry, and doubt, when all of a sudden, literally out of the blue . . .

"Santa's coming!"

Cameron, who was a year younger than the rest of my friends and therefore more prone to excitement over such things, was nearly breathless with the news.

"Yeah, we know, Cameron," Jimmy said, rolling his eyes. "In about a month."

"No!" Cameron insisted. "Today! Santa is coming today!"

I thought maybe Cameron was confused, so I tried to straighten him out.

"Yesterday was Thanksgiving," I said. "Santa doesn't come on Thanksgiving. He comes on Christmas, and that's still a few weeks—"

"I know all that!" Cameron said breathlessly. "I'm not dumb. But Santa is coming to Bountiful today! In a helicopter!"

Whoa. This sounded interesting. Santa? In Bountiful? In a helicopter?

TODAY???

"Santa doesn't fly in a helicopter," said Danny, ever the skeptic. "He flies in a sleigh, with reindeer. Everybody knows that."

"But think about it," I said, warming to the idea. "What does a sleigh need in order to land? It needs snow. Do you see any snow here today?"

Danny glanced around, but he didn't need to. It was an unusually warm day for late November. We were wearing just light jackets, and there wasn't a snow flurry in sight. He shook his head.

"So," I continued, "I think a helicopter makes sense. How else is Santa going to land if there isn't any snow?"

Cameron was so excited he was practically dancing in the street. Either that, or he really had to . . . you know . . .

"He's supposed to land at noon on the baseball field by the city park," Cameron said. "My mom said she'd take us down there if you guys want to go!"

If we want to go?! Cameron had to be kidding. How could

we *not* want to go? This was Santa, the jolly old big guy himself, famous in song and story! This was Superman, Batman, Mickey Mouse, and the Lone Ranger all rolled up into one stupendous, red-suited Christmas colossus! This was . . .

"Dumb," Danny said. "I'm not going."

"Me neither," said Jimmy.

"Me neither," said Johnny.

Cameron hesitated a second, then added, "Me neither."

What can I say? Cameron was a follower.

They all looked at me expectantly.

"I don't know," I said, hesitantly. "I mean, I don't . . . uh . . . you know . . . I mean, I'd kind of like to . . . you know . . ."

Just then a car horn sounded. It was my parents, just in time. They beckoned me, and I walked over to the Impala.

"We're going to do some shopping," Mom said. "You can play until lunch time, and then you need to go home to eat. There's a nice turkey sandwich in the fridge for you. If you want to play after lunch, just leave us a note telling us where you're going to be. Okay?"

"Can I come shopping with you?" I was hoping they would be shopping someplace close to the city park.

Mom smiled. "Now, you know you can't go shopping with us at Christmastime," she said, teasing. "You stay and have fun with your friends. We'll see you around dinner time."

"Okay," I said. "But if you take me, I promise not to—"

It was too late. Mom waved good-bye as Dad pulled away. So as I turned to face my friends, I knew what I had to do.

"Sorry," I said. "I've gotta go. See you guys later."

I hopped on Ol' Blue and started riding toward the city park. Yeah, I know—I didn't have permission to ride that far from home. But Mom hadn't actually said I couldn't go downtown—just that I couldn't go downtown with *them*. And I was pretty sure even Mom would understand why I had to see this particular Santa on this particular day. I just had to. I mean, I would write my usual letter to Santa, and I would probably sit on the respective laps of two or three different department store Santas (every kid knows it helps to let every possible Santa know what you want for Christmas—you never know which Santa is going to have the most direct pipeline of information to *the* Santa).

But this Santa was special. He had to be. The way I saw it, arriving in a helicopter was just one step and eight—nine if you count Rudolph—sets of antlers away from arriving in a reindeer-powered sleigh, which meant that if this Santa wasn't the *real* Santa, he was pretty darn close. And if Santa was going to come through with a sled for me, I was going to have to get as close to the source as I could possibly get.

Thankfully it was almost all downhill to the city park, so I got there quickly—and, it turned out, about an hour before Santa was supposed to arrive. There were only about twenty other people there when I arrived, so I figured to get a pretty good place in line. But soon that number grew to about two hundred. A girl in front of me was the first to hear the helicopter. A cheer erupted from the milling throng, as much from relieved parents as from enthusiastic children. The helicopter swooped close to the ground, hovering over the throne that had been erected on a temporary platform near the pitcher's mound. A rope ladder was thrown from the chopper, and a large, red-clad man with a white beard emerged and began climbing gingerly down.

My line buddies and I were going nuts. What an entrance! With our eyes carefully focused on Santa, none of us noticed how the ladder had drifted toward the bleachers. In fact, we didn't pay much attention to the location at all until Santa slammed against the rusty wire mesh backstop, dangled precariously for a moment, and then fell head-first about twenty-five feet, landing almost directly on home plate.

"Safe!" a man called out behind me. I think he was trying to be funny, but nobody laughed. Instead, we watched in silent horror as Santa lay on the ground, motionless. A bunch of grown-ups ran to assist him while dozens of children wondered if they had just witnessed the death of Christmas. After a few minutes, Santa was revived—much to our collective relief. Adults continued to huddle around him—talking, pointing, gesturing toward us kids. Finally they helped him to the throne, where he slumped into a groggy lump of red-and-white felt.

Slowly children began approaching Santa, who seemed to barely acknowledge them. As I got closer to the front of the line, I could see that blood was beginning to mat his beard. His eyes seemed bleary and unfocused, and his skin was pale and wet with perspiration. To be perfectly honest, he was a little scary-looking, even by department-store Santa standards. But I kept thinking about my Flexible Flyer sled, and I figured I'd kiss the creepy old elf on his bloody red lips if I thought it would do any good.

I was about third in line when the mother of one of the children in front of me had had enough. She stormed up to one of the men who seemed to be in charge. "This is crazy!" she said. "Look at him! The man is injured! He needs help!"

"I'm sure he'll be okay," the man in charge said, trying to calm her.

"He's *not* okay!" she said. "Look at him!"

"No, *you* look, lady," the man said. "We've got about two hundred kids here who will—"

"Who will have to go through the trauma of watching Santa Claus pass out if you don't get this man to a hospital," the woman said, completing the sentence in not quite the same way as the man in charge intended it. Several other parents who were close to the front took the woman's side. Santa, meanwhile, continued slumping in his chair, looking straight ahead, never once reacting to the discussion around him—unless you want to count the blood that started dribbling from his beard to the furry white trim of his jacket.

At last the man in charge relented, and Santa was escorted to a car and driven away. I don't remember hearing what happened to him after that. To be honest—and I really hate admitting this, but it's true—I don't remember caring what happened to him after that. It wasn't until years later that I started thinking about the courage of the woman who took a stand against cruelty and insensitivity. While hundreds of us could think only of what we wanted from Santa, one person was willing to look past the Santa suit and see another person's pain.

But sadly, I wasn't that one person. All I could think about was getting the message to Santa that I really, really, *really* needed a new Flexible Flyer sled for Christmas. And I needed to do it immediately—in case there was a sudden rash of dangled, dropped, or otherwise damaged Santas.

"Sam!"

I turned around to see Cameron, who was standing about ten feet behind me with his mother.

"How did you get down here?" he asked.

"I rode my bike," I said, trying to act as big and tough as you can look when you're standing in line to see Santa Claus.

"That's a long way to ride a bike," Cameron's mom said. "I'm surprised your parents let you ride this far."

"Oh, they let me ride anywhere I want to go," I lied, making a mental note to do everything I could to keep my mom away from Cameron's mom at church on Sunday. Then I looked at Cameron. "I thought you weren't going to come down here."

He looked a little embarrassed. "I changed my mind," he said, adding confidentially, "Don't tell the other guys, okay?"

"Okay," I promised. Cameron was too young to understand that the only way I could tell the guys about him coming to see Santa would be to tell them that I had come down too. So I would take Cameron's secret with me to my grave—or to Scout camp, whichever came first.

"Hey, we're going to go to the Five Points Mall," Cameron

said. "Mom says there's a Santa there today, too. You wanna come?"

"I don't know," I said, doing my best to downplay my enthusiasm for another shot at Santa. "I may hang around here for a while."

Cameron looked around to see if he was missing something. The park was pretty lifeless, with bare-limbed trees that had shed their colorful fall leaves, a few swings, a slide, and a whole bunch of dried-up lawn. He looked back at me.

"Well, okay," he said, shrugging his third-grade shoulders. "Maybe we'll see you later."

"Yeah," I said. "Maybe."

"You be careful on your bicycle!" Cameron's mom called out as the two of them began walking toward their car.

"Oh, sure," I said. "I'm always careful."

Another slight exaggeration of the truth. But she didn't have to know about the "Look, Ma, no hands!" thing Ol' Blue and I liked to do, did she?

The Five Points Mall—well, we liked to call it a mall; it was actually just a bunch of stores really close together—was on the other side of town, but it was a straight shot down Main Street. In fact, Main Street was one of the five streets that intersected there to create the name Five Points. And since I pretty much had to go back in that general direction to go home, it seemed entirely logical for me to stop by for a quick visit with Santa Claus there. Unfortunately, Cameron and I weren't the only ones thinking the Five Points Santa would be an adequate replacement for the helicopter-backstop Santa. It seemed that all two hundred of those who were behind me in line at the city park were now ahead of me in line at Five Points.

"Look at those twins sitting on Santa's lap," I overheard a woman ahead of me saying to her husband. "Aren't they adorable?"

Twins? On Santa's lap? Could it possibly be . . . ?

It was. Jimmy and Johnny were up there, each with an arm around Santa's neck, posing while their Mom took a picture with a Polaroid camera. Jimmy looked a little uncomfortable, admittedly, but Johnny was fully into it. You could just tell. I saw the flash, then I saw them hustle down off Santa's lap—but not before Johnny could whisper something into Santa's ear.

I felt as though I should say something to them, but what? As a believer, it didn't seem appropriate to ridicule their visit with Santa. I was standing in line to see Santa myself, wasn't I? Besides, I was the newcomer to the neighborhood—I wasn't secure enough in my social standing to take a shot when one was clearly appropriate. Maybe it would be enough to just let them know that I was there, and that I had seen them.

Cameron, however, had no such reservations.

"Hey, Jimmy!" he called out from his place in the line, about thirty people ahead of me. "I thought you said it was dumb to go see Santa!"

Jimmy flushed with a nine-year-old mix of embarrassment and rage. "I said it was dumb to go see that dumb old Santa at the dumb old city park," he said. "And it was! Look at what happened to him!"

I doubted that Jimmy had foreseen the whole backstop incident, but his point made sense in a weird, disjointed, fourth-grade sort of way, and I waited for Cameron's response.

"Yeah, well . . . he was . . . you know . . . the helicopter was cool . . . and . . . he had . . . you know . . . there was cool blood and stuff . . . and . . . um . . . yeah . . . well . . . so . . . we saw that . . . and . . . you know . . . it was . . . you know . . . cool . . . and stuff . . ."

Okay, so maybe third graders aren't much at snappy comebacks. The point was, Jimmy and Johnny had been seen, and they knew they had been seen. That was all that mattered to me. Clearly there would be no further discussion among my friends on the subject of Santa Claus—at least this year. I slipped behind the rather large mother in front of me and allowed them to pass without further comment from me.

It seemed as though I stood in that long line for hours, but I'm not really sure how long I was actually there. The fact is, there is Real Time and then there is Fourth Grader Standing in Line to See Santa Claus Time—and I'm not sure one has any real bearing on the other. But I was about seventh or eighth from the front, and the end of my wait was in sight when I felt a firm hand on my left shoulder. I looked up into flashing blue eyes and whitish reddish hair, a prominent Romanesque nose, and lips that were definitely *not* smiling.

"Dad!" I said, suddenly panicked.

"Come with me," Dad said as he turned and walked away.

"But, Dad, I'm almost to the front—"

"Come with me. Now!"

Dad didn't get mad very often. He wasn't around enough to get mad all that much. He traveled a lot on work and church assignments, which is why most of the discipline and correction around our house came from Mom—and she seemed only too happy to provide it. So when he did get angry, he had your complete and undivided attention.

And he had my attention that afternoon at Five Points—Santa Claus notwithstanding. With only a moment's hesitation I left my hard-earned place at the front of the line and followed my father to the bench where Mom was sitting.

I probably don't have to say this, but she wasn't smiling either.

"What are you doing here?" Mom wanted to know.

"I'm . . . uh . . . well, I was waiting in line to see Santa," I said.

"How did you get here?"

"Um . . . well . . . I . . . uh . . . rode my bike."

"You rode your bike all the way down here?"

I thought it best not to mention the side trip to the city park at this point.

"Yeah."

"By yourself?"

"Yeah."

"And who gave you permission to do this?" she asked.

"Um . . . no one," I said.

"Did you tell anyone that you were coming down here?"

"Um . . . no."

"So if you'd been in an accident or something, no one in the world would have any idea where you were—right?"

I was going to say something about God knowing where I was, but this didn't seem to be the time or the place for a philosophical discussion.

"No . . . I mean, yeah . . . I mean, right."

To this point, Dad hadn't said anything. He rarely did at such times. He left this part of family maintenance to Mom. But the look on his face was enough. I was in big trouble. *Big* trouble. I know this because Mom said so.

"You are in big trouble, young man."

See?

And Mom never lied about things like that. If she said you were in trouble, trouble was precisely the thing that you were in. I was suddenly grateful we were in a public place. Trouble—whatever that turned out to be—probably wouldn't rear its ugly head in public.

Probably.

"We'll deal with this at home," Mom said.

"Get your bike, and we'll load it in the back of the car," Dad said, turning to go.

"No," Mom said. "He can ride it home."

"But it's a long, uphill climb," Dad said. "It'll take him an hour."

"Exactly," Mom said. "Only it better take him less time than that." She looked at me. "You have thirty minutes to get home," she said. "You'd better get moving and moving fast. It's going to take you a while to get up that hill."

"But, Mom," I said. "I was almost to the front of the line. Can't I just . . ."

"No," Mom said emphatically. "Absolutely not. You go straight home. We'll meet you there."

"Besides," Dad said, "you probably don't want to talk to Santa right now."

"Why not?" I said as the tears started to form in my eyes.

"You're on his naughty list," Dad said. "Whatever it is you want, after today the answer would be no."

I don't mind telling you that I cried all the way home, as much from the sting of being on Santa's naughty list as from the burning in my legs, chest, and side as I tried to pump—and then walk—Ol' Blue up the hill. Being chubby and not in particularly good shape, I usually tried to avoid the east-west hills in the foothill community to which we had moved. It was a straight shot up the hill from Five Points to our house, but the hill was long and steep, and it was hard to maintain a good pace when I was fighting my tender emotions the whole way.

The thing is, I really hadn't intended to be disobedient. It's not like I thought it through and decided to take off and not tell anyone where I was going. It just . . . happened. I heard about Santa arriving by helicopter and . . . well, it just seemed like the thing to do. And then there was the whole backstop slam/bloody

Santa/substitute Santa at Five Points thing. It just took on a life of its own. What was I supposed to do—go home?

Well, yeah. Probably. But I didn't. I wasn't trying to be disrespectful to Mom and Dad and their rules. Heck, I didn't even *think* about Mom and Dad and their rules. I just wanted to talk to Santa. I *needed* to talk to Santa. And now I was on the naughty list. I didn't know if I could ever face him again.

Especially after the next Sunday.

We were sitting around the Sunday dinner table when Mom asked, "Sam, what did you learn today in Sunday School?"

I had to think quickly. Mom would not be pleased to know that Billy and I had skipped Sunday School to check out the first light snowstorm of the season—and my first snowstorm of any kind, ever. In fact, she would be downright angry—so angry that she might have a heart attack or something, especially after the bike/Santa fiasco. So actually, I figured I was doing Mom a favor by protecting her from the painful truth.

"We learned about David and Goliath," I fibbed. I was pretty sure we had talked about the Bible story sometime in the fairly recent past, so it seemed like a safe call.

"And what did you learn about David and Goliath?" she asked.

I knew I couldn't afford to pause or stammer. If you're going to lie, you have to act as though you know what you're talking about. So I forged ahead anxiously.

"We learned that Goliath was big," I said. "Really big. Bigger than Dad. Bigger than Wilt Chamberlain. Bigger than just about anyone who ever lived. Bigger than—"

"We get the idea," Mom said as everyone around the table looked up from their roast beef, mashed potatoes, and gravy to giggle. "What else did you learn?"

I started to squirm a little, trying desperately not to let my discomfort show.

"Well," I said, "we learned that David was . . . um . . . smaller. Not like an ant or a bug or a rabbit or anything like that. Not that small. Just . . . you know . . . smaller . . . like a little kid. Small like that. Smaller than Goliath."

"Uh-huh," my mother nodded. "So Goliath was big and David was small. Go on."

This was getting serious. I had about exhausted my supply of David and Goliath trivia.

"Well . . . uh . . . see, David had this slingshot . . . and . . . you know . . . he got a rock and hit Goliath . . . and . . . well . . . Goliath died . . . and . . . well, that's what happened."

I was feeling pretty good about my lie until Mom asked one more question: "Why?"

"What?"

"Why?" she repeated. "Why did he kill Goliath? That's an important part of the story."

"Why?"

"Yes—why?"

"Yeah, tell us, Sammy," Ann taunted. "Why did David kill Go-Lieth."

I was so distraught I missed the pun. I even forgot to slug Ann for calling me "Sammy," a nickname I detested.

"Well . . . um . . . it was because . . . uh . . . you know . . . David had . . . I mean, Goliath had . . . sort of . . . um . . . stolen the king's . . . you know . . . singing harp . . ."

"Nice try," Mom said as laughter erupted around the dinner table. "You're thinking of Jack and the beanstalk. Different giant."

I was getting desperate. "Um, I don't think Mrs. Whitney told us why he had to kill him."

"That's the first thing you've said that I believe," Mom said. "Mrs. Whitney didn't tell you that because she wasn't there. She was sick today. And guess who she asked to be the substitute teacher in your class?"

I had a sick feeling in the pit of my stomach, and it had nothing to do with the parsnips I had just forced down. Looking at the smiles bursting around the kitchen table, I knew the answer.

"I'll give you a hint," Mom continued. "It's the same person who knows that today's lesson was on Queen Esther."

In my mind I could see a big, black check mark being placed next to my name on Santa's naughty list—right there next to the other check mark that was already there from my misguided attempts to see Santa two days earlier. Two strikes against me in one weekend. One more strike and . . . I didn't even want to think about it. I mean, even Mickey Mantle struggles when he's down 0–2, doesn't he? And even though he's been in tough spots in World Series games and stuff, he's never experienced the pressure of knowing there's a Flexible Flyer sled hanging in the balance.

Chapter Four

Even for kids who have lived their entire lives in the mountains, the first snowfall of the season is exciting. Ask any schoolteacher, and they'll tell you: expect the kids to be a little . . . well . . . flaky when the first snowflakes hit the ground.

So you had to figure things might get a little wild the next Monday at school. Not only had we been away for the long Thanksgiving weekend, but we had experienced the winter's first measurable snowfall the day before. There wasn't a ton of snow on the ground Monday morning—only an inch or two fell, and most of it had melted away by the time I made my way up the hill to school. But there was still enough to make everyone fairly giddy with talk of sledding, skiing, and of course, Christmas.

For my part, you could take the excitement everyone else

was feeling and multiply it by at least a factor of seven. I must have seen snow previously, because I was actually born in a hospital just a few miles from where we were living. But we moved to Arizona when I was one, and we hadn't been back until . . . well, until now.

"Look at that, Mom!" I said as I finished my breakfast and prepared for the hike up the hill to school. "It's so . . . so . . . you know . . . cold!"

"Well, yes," Mom said while she was scurrying around the house to try to find where she had put the winter coats. "Cold is a major element of snow. You have to have one to have the other."

"And it's so slickery and slidey," I said. "Even the cars are sliding around in it."

"I think the word you're looking for is *slippery*," she said.

Actually, I preferred *slickery*, but I was too enchanted by the snow to argue.

"Max showed me how to make a snowball," I continued, leaving out the part explaining that he introduced me to snowballs in the traditional way: by hitting me in the back of the head with one. "He said that if you hold your snowball in your hands for a second it will melt a little and turn to ice. Doesn't that seem kind of funny? Why would melting them a little freeze them more? That doesn't make sense to me. But it works. Do you want me to show you?"

"Galoshes!" Mom suddenly exclaimed. "We didn't get you any galoshes!"

I had no idea what galoshes were, but just the sound of them was enough to convince me that I didn't want any part of them. Mom looked at the clock.

"Well, I don't have time to get anything for you now, so you'll have to wear your Keds today," she said. "Besides, it's mostly melted. Just stay out of the snow as much as you can, okay?"

Mom and I both knew that that wasn't going to happen. But as a mother, she was obliged to say it, just as I was obliged to give her an emphatic "Okay!" as I ran out the door and planted my black canvas U.S. Keds in the first small pile of snow I could find.

By the time I covered the two blocks to Valley View Elementary School, my feet were soaked and freezing cold, and my fingers were numb from the snowball I had been melting in my hand halfway up the hill. I intended to use it to pay my respects to the first of my friends that I saw in the school playground that morning (one of the things Max taught me about snowballing etiquette is that you usually throw snowballs at your friends or at girls—only rarely do you throw them at people who might be inclined to try to hurt you for hitting them). But by the time Danny was within range, the snowball had melted to next to nothing. Evidently there is a fine line between melting the snowball enough to turn it to ice and just melting it—period. Clearly I had much to learn about snow arts and crafts.

For example, shoes. When I got to the schoolyard, I noticed that most of my friends were wearing their Sunday shoes. Again, this seemed counter-intuitive to me. Sunday shoes usually had slick soles, which meant you would slip and slide in the snow. Inside my Keds, my feet were awfully cold; the canvas seemed to just suck in the cold dampness. But at least the soles provided some traction in the snow. When I asked Danny about it, he just smiled, pointed at the hill behind the school and told me to watch Jimmy, who was standing at the head of a line of boys at the top of the hill. He stood there for a moment, watching some kids at the bottom of the hill. All of a sudden he started running full speed down the hill, then he started just sliding down the hill—fast—like a skier, only without the skis. He slid all the way to the bottom and then quickly got out of the way of the next slider, who had fallen about three-quarters of the way down and was rolling and bouncing to the bottom.

"Jimmy is the best slider in the fourth grade," Danny said with respectful admiration. "He almost never falls. Johnny is pretty good, too. I can get going pretty fast, but I usually fall."

As we walked closer to the hill, I could see that brown grass was clearly visible on the hill on either side of the slide the boys were using, as if they had pushed snow over to pack down the trail. Parallel tracks had been worn into the snow where they placed their feet to slide, and it looked pretty shiny and icy at the bottom of the hill.

"Isn't this dangerous?" I asked a little nervously as we started working our way up the hill.

"Nah," Danny said. "Well, maybe a little. I've seen some guys take some pretty good falls. One kid got a bloody nose, and there was blood in the snow for days. It was cool!"

Yeah, I thought. Cool. So cool I probably would have felt a chill if my feet and hands weren't already frozen.

I didn't realize how high and steep the hill behind the school was until I was standing in line with the other boys waiting for my turn to slide down. "Maybe I should just watch for a while," I suggested to Danny. "I can learn by watching you guys, and then I can try it later."

"Nah," Danny said. "The best way to learn is to slide."

"But isn't there a smaller trail for me to learn on?"

"Yeah," Danny said, pointing toward the lower-grade playground with some contempt in his voice. "You can go over there, but . . ."

He didn't finish. He didn't need to. I understood the certainty of humiliation if I were to be caught in the lower-grade play area. We all did—especially after the Eric Butler incident (Eric was one of our classmates who continued to hang out in the lower grade play area for the first couple of weeks of fourth grade. Some fourth- and fifth-grade boys thought it inappropriate, and they decided to teach Eric some playground protocol by . . . well, I won't go into detail, but does the word *swirly* mean anything to you?). Even though it had only been a few months since we were lower-grade students ourselves, you just couldn't go there—no matter what.

(Sorry, Cameron.)

So I was stuck unless I stepped out of line and walked back down the hill, which would be infinitely more humiliating—and possibly more painful—than falling. When my turn came to slide, I braced myself as I had seen others do and started to run.

"Wait!"

I stopped running just as quickly as I had started. I assumed this was because of the quick grip action of my Keds, but in reality it probably had more to do with the fact that I wasn't really running all that fast to begin with.

"You can't slide," a fifth-grader behind me said, snarling derisively as only a fifth-grader can.

"Can too," Danny said in a voice and tone that suggested a lot more defiance and aggression than I was comfortable with.

"Can't," the fifth-grader replied. "He's wearing Keds. You can't slide in Keds. He'll dig up the slide."

Danny looked at my shoes. "He's right," he said. "We had to make that rule. Sorry."

"It's okay," I said, at once embarrassed and relieved. "I didn't know. I'll wear my Sunday shoes tomorrow."

"By tomorrow this will be grass again," another fifth-grader said. "What an idiot."

"He's new," Danny said. "He's never been in snow before."

"Well, let him go make snow angels with the girls and get out of our way so we can slide!"

"Okay, I'll go," I said. Actually, the thought of making snow angels was kind of appealing—especially if Rhonda was involved. I started walking down the slide.

"GET OFF THE SLIDE, IDIOT!"

I'm not exactly sure who shouted at me, but whoever it was,

their point was well-taken. I moved quickly off the slide and was walking down the hill to where the girls were playing when the school bell rang. Instinctively, I veered back toward the school, stepping across the slide just as the world's first three-hundred-pound fifth-grader came barreling down. Okay, so he probably wasn't actually three hundred pounds, but it sure felt like it when he slammed into me full force, sending both of us sprawling in the snow.

I was a little dazed, and it felt as though I had bumped my head pretty good, but otherwise I was okay. The fifth-grader, however, was on his hands and knees crying, with blood streaming from his nose onto the snow. Danny said the kid hit the back of my head face-first; the first teacher on the scene said it looked like the boy had a broken nose. Before I knew it, I was in the principal's office being lectured about the dangers of sliding down the hills behind the school.

"But I wasn't sliding," I protested. "They wouldn't let me slide because of my shoes."

"So you took it out on the next kid down the hill?" Principal Adams wanted to know.

"No!" I said. "I didn't do it on purpose! I was just walking down the hill and the bell rang and—"

"You were walking down the hill?" Principal Adams asked. "Do you really expect me to believe that? All of the other boys have already admitted they were sliding."

"I was going to," I said, "but my shoes were wrong."

"Uh-huh." The principal got up from behind his desk and

stepped out into the school's front office. After speaking to the school secretary he returned to where I was sitting. "We're going to have your mother come up here. We'll see if she can help us sort through this."

Well, okay. That was it. Not only would this be my third strike, but I was pretty sure that somewhere off in the distance I could hear the Pearly Gates squeaking closed to keep me out.

To her credit, Mom was pretty calm about the whole thing. I think my bursting into tears the moment I saw her had something to do with that. She explained to the principal that I was a gentle, timid boy (it took years for me to figure out that she was saying I was basically a chicken—which was true, but still not something you want people to be saying about you, especially your own mother), and she doubted that I would do something that painfully aggressive on purpose. She suggested that Danny be called in to verify my story—which, of course, he did.

And that was that. Sort of. As a result of the incident, Principal Adams decided to ban sliding on the schoolyard hills, and the boys all blamed me for taking away their favorite winter recess activity. And the kid with the broken nose vowed to break my neck—or some other body part, I can't remember for sure. So for the next few weeks, I spent most of my recesses at my desk, reading. But at least there weren't any more check marks by my name on Santa's naughty list.

At least, not yet.

The problem was, I still had the two. And I was pretty sure that really nice Christmas gifts, such as Flexible Flyer sleds, would be reserved for boys and girls whose names weren't on the naughty list at all and who had check marks by their names on the nice list. So it logically followed—at least, according to fourth-grade logic—that it wasn't enough to just not be naughty; I had to be good. In fact, I had to be so outstandingly good that Santa would be moved to erase the check marks and draw a line through my name on one list and move it to the other. And I had just four weeks in which to do it.

So I started doing everything I could think of to be good. I made my bed every morning without being asked. I took my turn doing dishes without whining. I ate my . . . shudder . . . squash. I dutifully played Ken to Ann's Barbie when her friends weren't around to play with her. I took out the garbage whenever I saw it needed to be emptied—Russians and Martians notwithstanding.

I don't know if Santa noticed my hard work and good behavior, but Mom did. And she just wanted to know one thing: "What's going on?"

"Um . . . well, I just took my bath," I said as I emerged from the steamy bathroom.

"I know," Mom said. "Why? I didn't tell you to take your bath."

"I know," I said. "But you were going to. You always do. So I just . . . did it."

She looked at me, a mix of curiosity and concern on her face.

"Uh-huh," she said. "So what are you up to?"

For the first time in my life, I felt guilty for having done nothing wrong.

"I just . . . you know . . . want to be . . . you know . . . good."

The light clicked on in Mom's mind. "Ahhh," she said. "I get it. It's Christmas, and you want to make sure you're on the nice list."

Oh, man. Was I that transparent?

"Well," I stammered, "yeah. I mean . . . sure, it's Christmas. But . . . well . . . it's okay to be good, isn't it?"

She smiled. "Sure," she said. "But it would be nice if you could keep this up after Christmas. I'm enjoying it!"

So simply being good wasn't enough. I had to do something great, something so spectacularly good that even Santa would notice—and overlook anything else he may have noted during the year.

That opportunity came the following Sunday when Mrs. Thacker stood in front of the congregation and asked for volunteers to help put on a special Nativity program at our church's annual Christmas party. She said she especially needed young people, and she promised significant blessings for all who participated. I wasn't exactly sure what constituted a "significant blessing," but I figured it could very well include turning naughty into nice—or a brand-new Flexible Flyer sled. So I signed up. Mrs. Thacker said she was very happy to have me in the program, because she had the perfect part for me.

A few days later at our first rehearsal, I found out what my "perfect part" was. I was supposed to walk to the center of the stage, with all the lights focused on me, and say boldly and with great feeling, "The Wise Men brought gifts to the baby Jesus: gold, frankincense, and myrrh."

Okay, so it wasn't a huge part. It was just one simple declarative sentence about the gifts of the Magi. And, yeah, I know it was historically inaccurate, since the Magi probably didn't arrive on the scene until sometime after Jesus was born, when He was more of a young child than a baby. But it was my line, my moment in the spotlight, and Mrs. Thacker said it was perfect for me. So I was prepared to milk it for all it was worth.

Especially if it was worth . . . you know . . .

I became especially excited about my line after our first rehearsal. I mistakenly pronounced the gifts as "gold, Frankenstein, and mirth" and had the whole cast laughing. It was an honest mistake—I really did think it was Frankenstein and mirth, along with the gold. To a nine-year-old boy, they seemed like pretty cool gifts. But everyone thought I was just being funny, and I became something of a folk hero onstage— the goofy new kid in the congregation who said "Frankenstein" instead of "frankincense." Every time I came out on stage, everyone paused to listen. They wanted to hear it if I messed it up again.

And I did—just to be funny. Several times.

But I knew better than to say "Frankenstein" during the actual performance of the pageant. For one thing, Paul, the teenager playing Joseph, threatened to beat me up if I did. And for another, Rhonda was going to be there. And nobody likes to look like a goofball in front of the girl he's trying to impress. You know what I mean?

On the night of our performance I walked around backstage repeating the word *frankincense* over and over again. Not only was I going to say it correctly, but I was going to say it with style. "Frankincense" was going to roll off my tongue as if I actually knew what it was . . . which I didn't. But that wasn't the issue. The issue was scoring a few "nice list" points while saving myself from a beating and making myself look good in front of Rhonda. And all that would be required to achieve all of that was a well-spoken multisyllabic word that sounded an awful lot like *Frankenstein*.

But wasn't.

As my big moment onstage approached, I was behind the curtain repeating the word: "Frankincense. Frankincense. Frankincense." It was still swirling in my mind as I approached the microphone. I could feel the warmth of the spotlight on my face and the whirling of butterflies in my stomach as I cleared my throat and spoke: "The Wise Men brought gifts to the baby Jesus: gold, frankincense, and . . ."

My mind went blank. I had spoken "frankincense" clearly. "Frankincense" was resonating all over the hall. But I couldn't for the life of me remember what came next. If I could have seen Mom, she would have mouthed the word to me. Heck, everyone in the gym knew what word came next—everyone, that is, except me. But with the spotlight glaring in my eyes, I couldn't see anyone in the darkness.

So I started over.

"The Wise Men brought gifts to the baby Jesus: gold, frankincense, and . . ."

Still nothing.

Total blank.

It was a short word—I knew that. One syllable. So I said the first short word that popped into my mind: "Nuts."

To this day I can't say that word—*nuts*—without feeling my ears burn with embarrassment. I can still hear the roar of the audience's laughter behind me as I hurried off the stage. I can still see Paul's icy glare from the Nativity scene. I can still feel the preadolescent heartbreak of Rhonda's post-production cold shoulder. And I can still almost taste the bitter disappointment of knowing deep in my soul that I had taken a mighty and sincere swing at doing good—at *being* good—and I had whiffed.

Strike three.

I was out.

Chapter Five

By the time I finally got around to seeing Santa Claus that Christmas, I had pretty much given up hope of finding a new Flexible Flyer sled under the tree on Christmas morning. In fact, I was angling for something—anything—besides the lump of coal that seemed to be inevitably headed my way. So I figured it was in my best interest to avoid seeing Santa at all. I had this vision of him pulling out his little black notebook, turning the pages, scanning for my name, and then looking at me disapprovingly.

"You're not on the nice list," he would say.

"I know," I would mutter, embarrassed.

"That means . . ."

"I know. Don't bother looking. Two check marks."

No doubt his white eyebrows would arch.

"Two?" he would ask.

"Two," I would reply.

"I see." He'd sigh, slip his notebook back into his pocket, and look me straight in the eye. "So will that be one lump, or two?"

Yeah, that's how it would play out. I was sure of it. So there wasn't really any point in putting either one of us through what was sure to be an awkward few minutes. I mean, it was hard enough to go up there and listen to the inevitable comment from some dorky elf about what a big boy I was. But it just wasn't worth it to go up there knowing perfectly well that there was a better chance of Marshall Dillon kissing Chester right on the lips than there was of me having a Flexible Flyer Christmas.

Still, I wasn't sure what to say when Mom confronted me three days before The Day.

"It's almost Christmas, and you haven't been to see Santa yet," she said.

"I know," I said, shrugging my shoulders. I was tempted to point out that I had *tried* to see Santa the day after Thanksgiving, but this didn't seem like the right time to remind her of that.

"Well, since tomorrow is Sunday, and Monday is Christmas Eve—and you know how busy Santa is on Christmas Eve— maybe we'd better get down to Five Points to see him today," she said.

I was torn. Part of me wanted to believe there was still the tiniest shred of hope. But the rest of me doubted . . . well, everything. I doubted Christmas. I doubted Santa. I doubted that there really was a red-nosed reindeer named Rudolph, a snowman named Frosty, or a partridge in a pear tree.

And I doubted me. I wasn't sure I could be on anybody's "good" list. I wasn't sure I deserved a Flexible Flyer sled. And even if I got one, I wasn't sure I could stay on it all the way down Mill Street to Orchard Drive. The only thing I was sure of was that Christmas would come and go, and that 1963 would be, for me, The Year of Drying Dishes.

"I don't know," I said at last.

"What do you mean, you don't know?" Mom asked.

"I don't know," I said. "I'm not sure . . . you know . . . about Santa . . . and everything."

"Well," she said, "what do you think?"

I paused. This was big. If I publicly proclaimed my doubt where those eavesdropping elves could hear me, I ran the risk of losing the last possible hope I had of ever flying down a hill on a Flexible Flyer sled. But if I didn't, Mom was going to make me go face the author of the naughty list himself.

"I think . . . um . . . well . . . I think . . . I sorta . . . you know . . . don't know."

Mom paused. This was big for her, too. I mean, it's not like she hadn't been through the Santa doubts with her other seven children. But this was it. I was her baby. The last believer. Heck, I was her "last" for a lot of things, from potty training to driver's training to going away to college. And through all my years of being her baby, she never let any "last" happen without putting up a fight.

"I'll tell you what," she said. "Let's go down to Five Points today and just see how things look. If you decide that you want to talk to Santa, you can. And if you decide that you don't . . . well, I guess that's okay, too."

So we went down, even though I was still apprehensive. I was actually leaning toward forgetting the whole thing until we walked into the mall and saw that the line was surprisingly short. And that Santa looked so kind and understanding and forgiving. And that I couldn't see any lists or coal or anything. And before I knew it, I was sitting on his lap.

"I was beginning to wonder if you were going to make it this year," Santa said.

Okay, that wasn't what I was expecting to hear from the old guy. I was expecting something along the lines of, "Ho, ho, ho, and what would you like for Christmas, little boy?" Or maybe, "Ho, ho, ho, have you been a good boy this year?" At the very least, I was definitely expecting a "Ho, ho, ho." What I wasn't expecting was a question like that. Like he knew me. Like he missed me. Like he knew that I was struggling this year. Like he was . . . was it possible? . . . the real, true Santa.

"I've been kinda . . . you know . . . busy," I said, regretting my words as soon as I said them. I mean, give me a break. I was nine and in the fourth grade and I was telling Santa Claus that I'd had a busy December?

Santa smiled playfully. "I understand," he said. "This is a busy time of year for everyone. So let's not waste time here. You've made a few mistakes this year, haven't you?"

Holy cow! Clearly, this was the real, one and only, true Santa. And he knew *everything*!

"Um . . . well . . . you know . . . there's this hill near my house called Mill Street . . . and the boys in my neighborhood are, you know, saying that I can't . . ."

"It's all right, son," Santa said, still smiling. "You don't need to explain. We all make mistakes. The important thing is that we learn from them. So what have you learned from your mistakes this year?"

This conversation was not going at all how I expected, so his questions were catching me completely unprepared.

"Well . . . not to . . . you know . . . lie and stuff . . ."

"That's a good thing to learn," Santa acknowledged. "What else?"

"Um . . . not to . . . you know . . . skip Sunday School and stuff . . ."

Santa looked at me with horror in his eyes. "You skipped Sunday School?" he asked, as if I had just confessed to putting grease on the wire for the Flying Wallendas.

"Only once," I insisted.

Okay, that's it! I thought. I'd just lied to Santa. I might as well go ahead and throw up on him now, just to ensure the delivery of what was sure to be a record cache of Christmas coal.

But Santa didn't seem to be fazed by it.

"I can live with once," he said. "As long as you don't do it again."

"Oh, I won't," I promised.

At least, not until the next Sunday snow storm, I thought.

"Well, all right, then," Santa said, glancing at the ever-growing line of last-minute lap-sitters behind me. "If that's the worst of it, I don't think we have to put your name on the naughty list. At least, not this year."

That's it? Just a simple—and not altogether complete or honest—confession, and I'm back in the running for real, actual Christmas presents? Part of me was thrilled. The other part of me wondered how it could possibly be that easy. I was too young to consider the theological implications of such extraordinary grace. I just knew that I deserved to be smitten with coal for Christmas—but according to Santa, I wouldn't be. I stood there, amazed. Overwhelmed. Dumbfounded—heavy emphasis on the "dumb."

"Aren't you forgetting something?" Santa asked as I slid off his lap and headed toward the elf who was handing out candy canes. I looked back at him vacantly, still trying to comprehend the incredible possibilities just reopened to me.

"Uh . . . thank you?"

Santa smiled. "You're welcome," he said as he pulled a squirmy little girl onto his lap. "But didn't you want to tell me what you want me to bring you for Christmas?"

Oh, yeah. That. Well, of course I did. That was the whole

point of coming here, wasn't it? I wanted him to bring me a . . . a . . .

My mind went blank. Absolutely, totally, completely blank. A bike? No, I got Ol' Blue last year. Lincoln logs? No—boring. An official Davy Crockett coonskin cap? Maybe.

"I . . . uh . . . don't really care," I blurted.

Well, at least I didn't say "nuts" this time.

"Good," Santa said. "Then you won't be disappointed with whatever I bring, will you?"

I nodded numbly and turned to go. In a blinding flash of smooth, varnished wood and bright red paint, I suddenly re-membered the sled and started back to tell him, but he was al-ready deeply involved in a conversation with a little girl who had—I'm not kidding—a fifty-seven-page list of instructions for the bearded old guy.

Well, okay—it was at least ten pages.

Or maybe two.

But seriously, there were a lot of things on that one-page, handwritten list. I promise.

And Santa was fully engaged in it. How could he not be? The little tyrant would reach up and put her hands on his cheeks and redirect his focus back to her if his eyes drifted at all. And if that wasn't bad enough, there were tons of other kids now awaiting their last shots at Santa. So there I was, in the middle of a mall that wasn't really a mall on the eve of Christmas Eve . . . er . . . eve, feeling almost as stupid as the stupid candy cane I was holding, having once again messed up an opportunity to talk to the one and only person to whom I could reasonably and honorably talk about the only thing I really, really wanted.

I began to believe in destiny—and clearly, I was destined *not* to have a Flexible Flyer sled for Christmas.

The last couple of days before Christmas probably would have been long and painful had they not been so darn interesting. First, Rhonda passed out in Sunday School. Right there, in front of God and everyone. Her mom was our teacher, which meant that the lesson was pretty much over at that point. Mrs. Whitney sent Billy and me out to get help while she worked to revive her daughter. And I'll be honest, it was kind of thrilling. Billy and I literally ran through the halls of the church, looking for someone who looked like they could help. Keep in mind that I still had a crush on Rhonda (something that would happen off and on throughout our growing-up years until we finally kissed on the night of our senior prom—and both started laughing at how silly it seemed to be romantically kissing one of your all-time best friends). I felt like a knight on a quest in behalf of his damsel in distress—until Jimmy and Johnny's dad suddenly appeared in the hallway and started chewing us out for running in the church. We breathlessly told him about our crisis, and being the good scoutmaster that he was, he ran to the classroom to help.

That's right—he ran. In the church. The very thing he had just yelled at us for. I would have chuckled at the irony if only I had known what irony meant—and if I weren't running right behind him trying to keep up.

Thankfully Rhonda was pretty much up and alert by the time we got back. Jimmy and Johnny's dad picked her up and carried her off, but not before she looked back over his shoulder and (I swear) actually gave me a weak smile as she left the room.

"Did you see that?" I whispered to Billy. "She smiled at me!"

"No—she smiled at *me!*" Billy insisted.

"Why would she smile at you?" I asked. "Isn't she your cousin or something?"

"Second cousin, once removed," he said, huffing as though he knew what that meant.

"So you're related," I said. "So you can't like her. That's in the commandments or the Beatitudes or something."

I was proud of what I thought was a terrific scriptural reference—especially since I had learned about the Beatitudes only a few weeks earlier in Sunday School. Billy heard about them too, but he hadn't paid any more attention to what they actually were than I had. Still, I had him over a barrel because he couldn't really argue the point with me. So he did the next best thing. He chomped on sour grapes.

"Well, I don't think she smiled anyway," he said. "I think maybe she had gas or something."

"That's dumb," I said. "Girls don't have gas."

"They do too!" Billy said.

"Do not!"

"Do too!"

"Do not!"

When you're in fourth grade, this is what is known as

"debating." And the Great Gas Debate continued all the way down the street as Billy and I walked home from Sunday School. I even brought it up for discussion around the Sunday dinner table.

"That's an inappropriate subject for the dinner table," Mom said as she passed me another roll in a not-so-subtle attempt to shut me up.

"I don't know," Dad said, impishness sparkling in his bright blue eyes. "You asked him what he learned in Sunday School today, and evidently this was an important part of the discussion."

"Besides," Linda added huffily, "everyone knows girls don't have gas—at least, not like boys."

"How can everyone know something that isn't true?" said my big brother Max, who at age eighteen considered himself to be an expert on pretty much everything.

Especially, it turns out, on gas.

This conversational thread continued throughout the rest of Sunday dinner, much to Mom's consternation and Dad's not-so-secret delight. For me, it was the most interesting Sunday dinner discussion we ever had and one of the reasons the day before the day before Christmas *passed*—if you'll pardon the expression—so pleasantly.

Christmas Eve dawned cold and snowy—the snowiest day of the season, which made it the snowiest day I had ever personally experienced. Mom said it was perfect for Christmas, and she threw herself joyfully into Christmas Eve baking and cooking, softly humming "White Christmas" nearly all day long.

"This is why we moved here," she said more than once during the day. "I've been dreaming of a white Christmas ever since we moved to Arizona seven years ago."

And white it most certainly was. Nearly a foot of snow covered the yard, driveway, and sidewalks, which Max was assigned to scrape clean whenever it snowed. As a result, Max had a slightly different perspective on the whole white Christmas thing.

"I don't know why we had to move here anyway," he said to no one in particular as he shoveled the driveway for the second time in the space of two hours. "I hate snow!"

I don't know why this particular moment seemed like the right time for me to show Max how much more proficient I had become in the wintery art of snowball making and throwing. It just did. I hit him square in the back with a snowball that had the perfect mix of ice and snow. Within startlingly few seconds, Max was introducing me to a new wintertime sensation: the fresh-snow face wash. He was just about to top off the face wash with a wickedly wild winter wedgie when Dad stepped out from the garage.

"Max, you're not picking on your little brother, are you?" he asked sternly.

"Uh . . . no," Max said, picking me out of the snow and ineffectually dusting the snow off of my parka. "We were just . . . you know . . . goofing around. Weren't we, Sam?"

I was young, but I wasn't so young that I didn't know that

there was only one correct answer to this question—even if it wasn't exactly the most accurate answer.

"Yeah," I agreed. "We're just . . . you know . . . goofing . . . you know . . . around."

"Well, you need to quit goofing around and get this driveway shoveled," Dad said to Max. Then he looked in my direction. "You come with me."

Dad said it with a degree of sharpness that made me think maybe I had done something wrong. My mind raced to consider the possibilities, but as I followed Dad into the garage, I couldn't for the life of me think of what it might have been. He stopped at his work bench, upon which lay a pile of metal and wood. Clearly whatever it had been was now broken beyond recognition, but I honestly couldn't remember having done anything so obviously destructive.

Dad turned to face me with a smile.

"Well, I think it's ready to go," he said, beaming. "Shall we try it out?"

Sure, I thought. *But what is it?*

Dad pulled the wooden . . . uh . . . *thing* off the bench and handed it to me. I studied it for a moment. It looked vaguely familiar, with its wood and rusty metal frame. Suddenly it dawned on me what it was—and what it definitely wasn't.

"I think we finally have enough snow," Dad continued as I gingerly held the . . . well . . . the object in my arms. "Let's take Old Betsy out for a spin!"

Old Betsy? I thought, horrified at the implications. Not only was it the ugliest piece of snow-riding equipment ever created, but it was named for an elderly pioneer woman! How was I going to explain *that* to my friends?

"No," I would say at the top of Mill Street Christmas morning, "I don't have a Flexible Flyer. But I do have Old Betsy here!"

They'd laugh me all the way to Orchard Drive.

And back.

Still, it was difficult to resist Dad's enthusiasm—he hadn't been named Top Salesman in three western states for nothing. And he *had* invested some time and energy in trying to fix the sled, although it should be noted that Dad was sort of the Clem Kadiddlehopper of home repairs—just like Red Skelton's lovable knave, his big heart was in the right place, but his fingers and hands rarely were, which meant his repair projects often ended up doing more harm than good.

I was taking all of this into account as Dad and I stood on top of the highest, steepest slope on the hill just behind the elementary school.

"There's nothing to it—honest," Dad said, trying to coach—and coax—me into taking that first slide down the hill. "You just push the sled and run alongside it until you feel like you've got enough speed going then you hop on it and . . ."

"And, what?" I asked. "That's the part I don't get. What do you do when you're on it?"

Dad paused for a moment. I don't know if he was contemplating the possibilities or if he couldn't believe that his youngest son didn't understand gravity.

"You . . . you just . . . hang on to the handles and you . . . you just ride it down the hill," he said at last. "Of course, you can steer it by twisting this bar here one way or the other . . ."

He tugged at the crossbar at the top of the sled to illustrate. It broke.

Dad held the rotted piece of wood in his hand. Then he looked at me. "Okay, so you won't steer," he said, enthusiastically. "Steering is overrated as far as sleds are concerned. You really don't steer them all that much, and on an icy hill, the steering mechanism on a sled is pretty much useless."

"Jimmy said you have to steer in order to ride all the way down Mill Street to Orchard Drive," I said. "He said if you don't steer, you'll end up in the Kimball's pyracantha bushes."

"Well, I don't think you should be sledding down Mill Street anyway," Dad said. "That's much too dangerous, with all the cars and everything. You should just sled here, where there are no cars and the hill is long and straight."

And boring, I thought.

Still, for a first-timer, the hill behind the school was probably a good idea. To be perfectly honest, I was kind of relieved not to be making my first sled run in front of my friends. And who knew? Maybe this unsightly little sled would turn out to be a flash of lightning on the snow.

Hey! That was a good name: *Flash!* That's what I'd call it. Not Old Betsy. Flash! Like the Scarlet Speedster in the comics. Flash was all about speed, wasn't he? SUPER-speed, in fact.

And maybe my beat-up little sled—my Flash—would be about speed, too, even if he wasn't much to look at.

With a firm hand and grim determination, I grasped the sled by its time-worn edges and moved as fast as my chubby legs could carry me through a foot of snow. I bent low, as my father had suggested, and started pushing the sled down the hill. When Dad shouted, "Now!" I flopped belly down onto the sled and held on for dear life. For a moment I felt the wind on my face and the slight sting of snow as it whipped up from the ground into my eyes. It didn't really feel like I was going all that fast, but I was sure I was. I could hear the snow crunching under Flash's runners, then an ominous-sounding grinding noise, then silence. Stillness. As if I were suddenly airborne. Or perhaps . . . just . . .

Stopped.

Halfway down the hill.

Flash was just stuck there—my feet pointed up, my head pointed down. I hadn't conquered the hill, but evidently I had overcome gravity and several laws of physics that I wouldn't even know existed until my third year of college.

"What are you doing?" Dad bellowed from the top of the hill.

"I don't know!" I shouted back, not daring to move in case Flash decided to . . . you know . . . flash on down the hill. "It just . . . stopped!"

"Well, what did you do?" Dad wanted to know.

"I didn't do anything!"

"You must have done *something*," he shouted as he started down the hill toward me. "Sleds don't just stop halfway down snowy—"

Suddenly Dad's feet slipped on the snowy hill, and he went down, head first, sliding on his tummy almost all the way to the bottom of the hill.

This was embarrassing. My fifty-two-year-old father could slide down the hill on his tummy farther and faster than I could on my sled. This did not bode well for my future as neighborhood sledding champion. I was prepared to battle Old Lady Morgan, pyracantha bushes, cynical friends, and traffic on Orchard Drive. I was not prepared to battle nature itself.

"Let me take a look at that thing," Dad huffed as he trudged back up the hill to where I was still prone on the sled. "I'm sure there's a simple explanation . . ."

I started rolling off the sled just as Dad reached for the frame. Unfortunately, I was still partially on Flash as Dad started to lift, and the combination of his strength and my weight was more than the little sled could bear. The part that Dad was lifting on . . . well . . . it lifted. But the part I was still lying on stayed under me. On the ground.

Suddenly we had the world's first pop-top convertible sled.

For a moment Dad just looked at the splintery wood in his hand. Then he looked at me.

"This isn't as bad as it looks," he said.

I was relieved to hear that, because from where I was lying in the snow, it looked awful.

"I've got some wood at home that I think will work nicely in this area here," he said, pointing to the area just vacated by the wood in his hand. "A little sanding and a few screws and it'll be good as new. Then I'll just file some of the rust off the runners and give them a good coat of paraffin wax, and you'll have the best-looking, fastest sled in the neighborhood."

You had to love that about my Dad—he was always positive. But somehow I wasn't feeling especially positive as we trudged down the hill and across the field toward home, carrying in our hands the battered, broken fragments of my last chance at acceptance.

Chapter Six

I should have been expecting it.

I mean, it's not like I hadn't experienced it every single Christmas Eve. But I was so absorbed in my sledding traumas and tragedies that I walked into the house that afternoon completely unprepared.

"Oh, man!" I said, wincing at the pungent odor. "Who died?"

"About a million oysters," Ann said, as smart-alecky as a twelve-year-old girl can sound when she's doing all her breathing out of her mouth. "It's Christmas Eve, remember?"

My heart and my stomach sank, simultaneously.

I'm not sure how oyster stew became a Christmas Eve tradition at our house. We're not big oyster eaters. Never have been, as far as I know. I don't remember ever going to our favorite seafood restaurant, Bratten's Grotto, and having anyone order anything having to do with oysters—no oysters Rockefeller, no oysters on a half shell, no oysters Kilpatrick, and no oyster stew (I did like oyster crackers in my Campbell's tomato soup, but I don't think that counts). The closest we got was when Mom and Dad would order Bratten's clam chowder, which I guess is kind of like oyster stew, only without the oysters. Or the stew.

But every Christmas Eve we were up to our elbows in the gooey, smelly stuff because . . . well, just because.

"Oyster stew is the traditional Christmas Eve meal," Mom said in a tone that suggested her word on the subject should be enough. But Max was just a month away from leaving home, and he was willing—even eager—to push at the boundaries a bit. Just for fun.

"But whose tradition is it?" he asked from the kitchen doorway as Mom put the finishing touches on the homemade rolls that would accompany the stew. "I mean, I don't know anyone else who has oyster stew on Christmas Eve. I asked my friends, and none of them have heard of it. Up at the Millers they're having prime rib—that's *their* Christmas Eve tradition."

"We should have that tradition, Mama," Ann said. "I like prime rib."

Mom glared at her youngest daughter. "You've never *had* prime rib," she said.

"I know," Ann said as she continued putting the nice

silverware on the dinner table. "But it sounds good. Better than oyster stew."

"I'm just trying to understand," Max pressed, fully aware of how close he was to pushing Mom into full Christmas Eve meltdown—another holiday tradition around our house, as I recall. "I can see the reason behind the other Christmas traditions. They either have something to do with Jesus or Santa. But I can't see a Jesus or Santa connection to oyster stew."

Mom never pretended to be a scholar. Like many who grew up during the Great Depression, she went right to work to help support her family after graduating from high school. She always felt a little inadequate intellectually, and she hated it when she felt her children were trying to take advantage of her lack of education—almost as much as she hated it on those rare occasions when we complained about something she was cooking.

"I'm sure they ate something like oyster stew in Jesus' time," Mom said huffily.

"Maybe the Romans did, but not the Jews," Max said authoritatively. "I don't think Jews can eat oysters. It's a shellfish, and I'm pretty sure that shellfish are on the list of things that Jews can't eat."

Mom gave the stew one last angry stir and slammed the lid back on the pot. "Then maybe you'd like to find a nice Jewish family who you can have Christmas Eve dinner with tonight!"

This was the point at which Max needed to stop and apologize. We all knew that. When Mom got close to tears, you needed to back off or risk a long and painful period of retribution—not to mention Dad's wrath. But Max had her cornered on this subject, and he knew it. He just couldn't resist one last dig. "Um . . . actually . . . I don't think Jews observe Christmas Eve . . . or Christmas—"

Mom whirled to face Max squarely, tears beginning to well up in her eyes. "Why are you doing this?" she asked, her voice choked with emotion. "This is our last Christmas with you home, and you're ruining it!"

Max tried to retreat, but was weak and too late. "I'm not ruining . . . I just . . . you know . . . wondered . . ."

Mom wiped her hands on her apron and stormed out of the kitchen just as Dad walked in the back door, snowflakes still clinging to his shoulders and red hair.

"That oyster stew smells delicious!" he said enthusiastically. "When do we eat?"

Mom was almost to her bedroom by now. "Ask your son!" she snapped over her shoulder. "He seems to know everything about it!" And then her bedroom door slammed shut.

Dad stood in the doorway for a moment, trying to get his emotional bearings. He looked at Max and then at me. "Would one of you care to explain to me what's going on?" he asked.

I looked at Max helplessly. I didn't want to rat out my big brother, but I couldn't take the risk of another check mark on the naughty list so close to Christmas morning.

"It was Max," said Ann, who never in her twelve years had passed on an opportunity to tattle. "He made Mama feel bad about cooking oyster stew, even though we all hate it."

You know, sometimes I really loved her!

"I didn't mean to make her feel bad," Max said quietly. "I was just . . . you know . . . kidding around. Teasing, mostly."

Dad looked at his newly adult son. "Uh-huh," he said evenly. "And we all know how much your mother likes to be teased—especially when it comes to the meals she works so hard to prepare for us."

Max's eyes dropped to the ground. "I know," he said. "I'm sorry."

"Well, don't tell *me*," Dad said. "Tell her."

Max looked toward Mom's bedroom door. "I will," he said. "Right after dinner."

"You'll do it right now or there won't *be* any dinner—for any of us!" Dad said.

Max looked at Linda, Ann, and me helplessly. Then he moved slowly toward Mom's bedroom, pausing to look back at us with his bravest and best we-who-are-about-to-die-salute-you smile, then he knocked on the door and went in. Dad waited for a few minutes, then he followed Max into the bedroom.

I'm not sure how long they were in there. To be honest, I took advantage of the opportunity to grab a handful of Christmas cookies and go downstairs for a little unsupervised TV. Three whole channels, all to myself! And cookies to stave off the hunger I would feel because I wasn't about to eat any of that—shudder!—oyster stew.

I was just settling into a special Christmas episode of *The Rifleman*—and my fourth cookie—when I heard Ann's scream.

"The kitchen's on fire! The kitchen's on fire!"

I ran up the stairs as fast as my chubby legs could carry me, arriving at the landing just as Dad, Max, and Mom barreled into the kitchen, which was now filled with thick, acrid smoke.

"Wanda, take the kids out of the house!" Dad barked. For once, Mom didn't question. She grabbed Ann and me by the neck and ushered us quickly into the backyard, with Linda following right behind. Max stayed in the house with Dad to do battle with whatever it was that was causing all that smoke.

We stood outside in the falling snow for a few minutes, shivering with fear as well as from the cold, until Dad burst out of the back door carrying a blackened pot that was billowing smoke. He threw the entire pot into a snow bank and began covering it with snow until the billowing and sizzling stopped.

"The oyster stew!" Mom gasped as the black lump of goo inside the pot gave one last hideous gurgle. "I thought . . . Linda . . . Max . . . Mike . . ." Mom was so desperate to find someone else to blame for an unprecedented second food disaster in less than a month (the first, the Thanksgiving chicken gravy conflagration, was *clearly* Dad's fault) that she even invoked the name of my big brother, Mike, the family's foremost mischief maker, whom Mom had once blamed for an actual, real-live earthquake when the family lived in Seattle. But Mike was doing missionary work for our church in New England and probably couldn't be blamed for anything west of . . . oh, say, Missouri.

No, Mom was going to have to take responsibility for this one. And she did.

"I guess I forgot about the oyster stew while we were talking about . . . well . . . the oyster stew," she said. "I'm sorry—it looks like I've ruined our Christmas Eve dinner."

"Nonsense!" Dad said. "The house is full of food. In fact, there's something I've been saving for a special occasion, and I think now is the perfect time."

We all moved back into the house, opening every window to let the smoke and odor out and the cold winter air in, while Dad disappeared into the basement. He emerged moments later carrying a sizeable box wrapped in festive red-and-green paper.

"This is from my father," he said as he began tugging at the ribbons and wrapping paper. "I already know what it is because . . . well, I helped him order one for each of his sons—including me!"

Soon I was regretting that fourth cookie as I recognized the familiar Swiss Colony box. It was a big one, filled with meats and cheeses and nuts and petit fours and, my personal favorite, chocolate fudge torte. This was the good stuff, and Dad wanted to make a meal of it.

"Those are just snack foods," Mom said. "That can't be our Christmas Eve meal."

"Why not?" Dad—and the rest of us—wanted to know. "We've got every food group covered. There's a beef log—that's the meat group. And cheese—that's dairy."

"And crackers," Linda said. "That's the grain group."

"And chocolate is a food group all by itself, isn't it?" Max asked.

"But there are no fruits or vegetables," Mom said. "We need something healthy with this."

"There's mustard," Ann said. "Isn't mustard a vegetable?"

"No," Mom said, warming to the gastronomical adventure. "But we've got mustard pickles, and pickles are made from cucumbers, and cucumbers are definitely a vegetable!"

"And we've got olives," Max added. "Are olives a fruit or a vegetable?"

Mom thought for a moment. "They're a fruit, I think," she said. "They have a pit, so I think that makes them a fruit."

"And they're green, so that means they're healthy, right?" I said.

"*Healthy* probably isn't the right word," Mom said, smiling. "I think *good* is probably a better word. Olives are definitely good! And we've got green ones and black ones on the storage shelves downstairs. Would you go get me a can of each?"

And the Andrews Family Christmas Eve Feast was on!

I wish I could tell you that from that point on we always had cheese balls and beef log for our Christmas Eve dinner. But Mom did start to break out the Swiss Colony as an appetizer, which made the annual oyster stew a little easier to take.

But oyster stew was a tradition, and as far as Mom was concerned, tradition must be served—especially at Christmas. No artificial trees, no "Blue Christmas"-themed house lighting, no modernistic Nativity displays. And there would positively be no rocking around our Christmas tree, no matter how popular the Brenda Lee song was that year. Traditional Christmas music was the only vinyl spinning on our hi-fi. Bing Crosby, Nat King Cole, Burl Ives, Percy Faith, Andy Williams, and the Mormon Tabernacle Choir were the order of the day, every day, from Thanksgiving to Christmas.

Tradition similarly dictated the rest of our Christmas Eve activities. After the Swiss Colony leftovers were put away and the pine-scented Glade mist air freshener had eliminated most (but not all) of the burnt oyster stew fragrance, we moved into the front room for our traditional Christmas Eve program. Max built a fire in the fireplace ("Next year," he told me, "this will be your job"), and we all sang "Away in a Manger." Then Dad read the Christmas story from the Bible, with Ann and I acting out the parts of Mary and Joseph, Max as the donkey, and Linda as various and sundry angels, shepherds, and innkeepers (this tradition was much more realistic and entertaining when there were eight children at home to play all of the parts). Then we sang "Silent Night" and had family prayer to conclude the "spiritual" portion of the program.

From that point on it was all about Santa. We put out our Christmas stockings on the furniture so Santa would have a place to put the presents he would bring to us (evidently, Ann was expecting quite a haul—"I've been very good this year," she said—so she kept the entire loveseat all for herself, while Linda, Max, and I had to share the couch). Then we picked out the best of the Christmas cookies for Santa and put them out next to the fireplace with a little mug of Meadow Gold Dairy egg nog.

"Don't forget to put the fire out before you go to bed," I told Dad.

"I won't forget," Dad said, smiling. "By the way, I never did hear what you are expecting Santa to bring you this year."

I paused. At this point it was too late to say anything that would make a difference; Santa's sleigh was loaded. Whatever I was going to get was already on its way. And I didn't want to make Dad feel bad about the old sled he had fixed for me—well, *sort of* fixed. "I told Santa that I didn't really care—whatever he wanted to bring would be fine," I said, and I couldn't help feeling a little melancholy when I said it.

"It's like in the song," Ann said as she was arranging her fourth stocking on the loveseat. Then she sang,

As for me my little brain isn't very bright.
Choose for me, dear Santa Claus,
What you think is right.

Then she added, "Especially the part about your little brain not being very bright."

Those were fighting words, and under normal circumstances, I probably would have gone after her. But I just wasn't in the mood. Not that I was sad or upset or anything. It was Christmas Eve, and I wasn't on the naughty list. So Santa was bringing *something*, and it would be something good, for sure. I just had no idea what it would be, so I didn't know how excited to get.

Or not.

Chapter Seven

The good thing about my pleasantly ambivalent feelings that Christmas Eve—besides keeping me from decking Ann—was that I had no problem getting to sleep that night. Usually I was so excited that I tossed and turned into the wee hours of Christmas morning; I can remember more than one Christmas Eve when I didn't sleep all night long. But this year was different—at least, until midnight, when Max came downstairs and woke me up.

"Hey, Sammy," he said as he shook me gently. "Wake up! It's Christmas!"

"I'm tired!" I said, my eyes barely open. "And it's still dark out!"

"Well, it's just *barely* Christmas," Max said. "But Santa has already come! Your presents are upstairs!"

Now he had my full attention.

"Santa came?" I asked, sitting up and rubbing my eyes. "And there are presents?"

"There sure are!" Max said. "And there's something pretty exciting up there for you!"

My heart started pounding. My fingers started trembling. I started feeling that old, familiar Christmas morning feeling.

"Here, look!" Max said. "I took a picture of it!"

He flashed a Polaroid print in front of my face so quickly that I didn't have time to focus on anything. The only thing I could make out was a flash of red. Whatever it was, at least part of it was red.

"Let me see that!" I said, reaching for the photograph.

"I can't," Max said, holding me off with one hand while brandishing the photograph with the other. "It wouldn't be right. You'll have to check with Mom and Dad to see if it's okay to go in and open our presents now."

That seemed like a good idea at the moment. It turned out not to be. I knocked softly on their bedroom door. The response was immediate.

"It's just barely past midnight!"

I wasn't exactly sure if it was Mom or Dad making that exclamatory observation. The voice was sleepy and angry and pretty much indistinguishable. But the message was clear.

"So I'm a little early?" I asked tentatively.

"You're a *lot* early," said The Voice.

"Okay, I'll check back in a couple of hours."

"Check back in about seven hours."

"Seven?"

"Yes," The Voice confirmed. "Seven. Seven A.M. No earlier. Got it?"

"Got it," I said, absolutely confident that I would die of old age before seven o'clock in the morning rolled around. I took one last shot. "But Max said there are presents—"

"Seven o'clock!" The Voice barked. "Now get back to bed!"

I turned slowly and started to back away from the door.

"But . . . Max showed me a picture—"

"Good night, Sam!"

"But I saw . . . red . . ."

"Samuel!"

I knew that tone, and I knew what it meant when they used my Bible name. It meant the conversation was over . . . as would be my young life if I uttered another syllable. So I left their door and headed down the hall toward the basement stairs, pausing for a moment—maybe two—to flirt with an attractive siren named Temptation, who—I swear to you—tried to talk me into going into the front room to take a peek for myself.

"Sammy Andrews," she sang in a voice that sounded an awful lot like Shelley Fabares singing "Johnny Angel." *"How you'll love it. And there's part of it that's shiny red . . ."*

I'll admit I even took a step—maybe two—down the hall. But I couldn't get past the possible long-term consequences of having Mom discover that I'd peeked. And she *would* discover it—make no mistake about it. She always found out about the dumb stuff I did. And the implications of this particular discovery were just too horrible to imagine. So I headed back down the stairs to begin a night-long vigil.

Flash of red? I wondered as I lay on my bed in the darkened basement. It could be a new bike. But I just got Ol' Blue last year, and he was still in good shape, and I actually kind of liked him, so I hoped it wasn't a new bike. It could be a train set—I'd always wanted an electric train set—and maybe one or two of the cars were red. I toyed with the idea that it might be one of those really cool erector sets, but I couldn't think of anything that would be red on one of those.

Or it could be King Zor, the Fighting Dinosaur. King Zor was cool—I had seen him on TV. He was motorized, and he even came with a dart gun (batteries, however, were *not* included). He would creep around while you set yourself up for a shot at the target that was attached to his tail. When you hit his tail, he whirled around toward you and started shooting these little Ping-Pong balls at you out of a launching site located on his back (evidently Ping-Pong has been around a lot longer than any of us thought). And I was almost positive that the target on King Zor's tail was a bright, shiny red (although it was difficult to tell for sure on our black-and-white Motorola set—but King Zor's tail target appeared on our TV to be the exact same shade of fuzzy gray as Donald Duck's bowtie, and I knew Donald Duck's bowtie was red—most of the time).

By the time my alarm clock said 6:45, I had pretty much convinced myself that I was about to do battle with King Zor, the

Fighting Dinosaur. And I was excited about it. I could improve my aim with the dart gun and my agility by dodging Ping-Pong balls as they fired at me. And it was the kind of toy I could play with by myself, which I would probably be doing—a lot—after my friends decided I was a total drip when I didn't get the sled that I'd told them I was *definitely* going to get.

"Hey! Get up! It's Christmas!"

Ann's half-whispered, half-shouted call to Christmas echoed down the stairs.

"But Mom and Dad said don't get them up until seven!" I called back, unwilling to incur any parental wrath for the sake of fifteen measly minutes.

"It's okay," Ann said. "We're all going to wake them up together. They can't get mad at *all* of us!"

Actually, I was pretty sure that they *could*. But I wasn't going to argue with anyone who was trying to get me into the front room—and into my first duel with King Zor—sooner. We lined up outside Mom and Dad's room, and on Max's count of three we all shouted as loudly as we could: "Good morning, Mom! Good morning, Dad! Merry Christmas!"

I stepped slightly behind Max. Okay, let's be honest. I was hiding behind my big brother. After my experience with The Voice a few hours earlier, I didn't want to appear to be a ring-leader in this.

I needn't have worried. Dad invited us into their room, where their bed was already made and Dad was dressed. Mom was still in her robe, but she was in the bathroom fixing her hair.

They were happy and pleasant and excited—a far cry from the fierce, nameless, faceless entity I had encountered fewer than seven hours earlier.

"But," Mom said, "before we go in . . ."

We all knew what was coming. Mom had this thing about how we needed to eat something solid before we started opening Christmas presents. I'm sure that somewhere in our family history there is a sordid story about some child somewhere getting violently ill after introducing Christmas stocking candy to an empty stomach. So every Christmas morning, Mom made sure we ate some toast and orange juice before we did anything else. The thing was, we all choked it down as fast as we could so we could get in to the presents, so it probably ended up doing us more harm than good. But we ate it just the same—as if we had any choice in the matter.

With the toast and orange juice out of the way, there was only one family Christmas tradition left through which to wade: lining up for the family march into the front room where the presents awaited. This was probably my favorite family tradition, because it required that we line up youngest to oldest. I liked that. It meant that I would lead the family into the room where Santa's deposit had been made, and I would therefore be the first one to see my new . . .

Barbie car?!

I blinked my eyes to make sure I was seeing things correctly as I warily approached the couch. Maybe the Christmas tree lights were playing tricks on me. Maybe the flashes of Dad's

Polaroid had distorted my vision. But no, there it was, right where I had placed my stocking the night before: a shiny, pink plastic convertible Austin Healy for Barbie. I stood over it for a moment, dumbfounded. *This is what happens when you're not specific with Santa,* I thought. My eyes wandered over the other presents near my stuffed stocking: a new dark-haired Barbie, a new Ken doll with painted-on hair, a big case to carry Barbie and Ken and all their clothes . . .

Something was wrong here. Something was terribly, terribly wrong.

"Hey, I didn't ask for a big, dumb old dinosaur . . ."

Ann's whine was unmistakable—and strangely comforting. I turned to look at where her toys were supposed to be situated on the loveseat, and there was King Zor, the Fighting Dinosaur, with his green plastic body and red tongue and tail target, poised and ready to turn Barbie's convertible into so much plastic mulch.

"It looks like Santa switched places for you two," Dad said.

"Well, why would he do a dumb thing like that?" Ann wanted to know.

"I don't know," Dad said. "I don't think it's a big deal."

"Well, that was my place, and I don't know why he would . . . oh, look! A Barbie car! And it's pink! And shiny!"

Thankfully, it didn't take much to divert Ann's attention. She moved immediately to her new Barbie stuff while I moved to the loveseat to check out King Zor—and to figure out how I could use my new Christmas toy to trash Barbie, Ken, their car, and all their little plastic accessories.

"Hey, that's cool," Max said as he reached for the green dart gun that was resting on the wooden shelf next to King Zor. "How does it work?"

"Well, on the commercial he goes forward until you hit that target on his tail with a dart, then he turns toward you and starts firing these Ping-Pong balls at you," I explained as I gently lifted the king from his perch on the shelf and positioned him on the floor, aimed directly at that shiny, pink car.

"What Ping-Pong balls?" Max asked.

"They're right there—on the shelf next to the darts," I said. I found Zor's on-off switch and pushed it to "on." He roared to life and started moving threateningly toward Barbie.

"Uh . . . Sammy," Max said hesitantly. "That isn't a shelf."

"Okay, that shelf or box or whatever it is," I said. "Watch this! King Zor is going to crunch Barbie's car!"

"You'd better not!" Ann warned.

"Hey, I can't control the king," I said. "You're going to have to hit his tail with a dart to make him turn!"

"Why don't I just hit *you?*"

"Sammy, look," Max said, tugging on my shirt to get my attention. "There's writing on the wood. In red. Can you read it?"

"Yeah, I'll look at it in a sec," I said, not taking my eyes off of King Zor as he made his ponderous way steadily toward the pink car. "I've gotta see this . . ."

"Mom!" Ann called. "Sam's dinosaur is going to crash my new car!"

"Sam, don't let your dinosaur hit Ann's car," Mom said in a tone that was only marginally threatening.

"It won't hurt it," I said. "I don't think . . ."

"Let's see," Max said behind me. "I can't quite make out that first word. I think it says 'Flexible' . . . 'Flexible' something . . ."

"Probably 'Flexible Flyer,'" I said absently, still focused on the carnage I was hoping I was about to see. "That's the best kind of sled there is."

"Yep, that's what it says," Max confirmed. "'Flexible Flyer.' Right there on that wooden whatever-it-is."

King Zor was just inches from the pink Austin Healy when it dawned on me what Max was saying. I whirled to face him.

"You got a Flexible Flyer for Christmas?" I asked incredulously.

"No," Max said, sitting on the floor next to the "shelf" that I could now see had bright red runners underneath it. "*You* did!"

For the first time in my life, I went completely numb (not counting the times when I was little and fell on my head and stopped breathing, which evidently was what entertained my brothers and sisters before we had a television in the house). I looked at Max. I looked at the "shelf." I read the words "Flexible Flyer" written in block white letters across a bright-red banner that appeared to be billowing behind a proud American eagle spreading its wings. I was so mesmerized by the sight that I swear I didn't even hear Ann scream when King Zor rammed her

Barbie car—or when she smacked the dinosaur's tail and got pelted with Ping-Pong balls.

I missed all of that. I was lost in what seemed like a dream as I reached out my hand and caressed the fine, varnished wood of the Flexible Flyer sled. I gently removed my stocking, a pair of new jeans, and a package of new underwear from the surface, paying absolutely no attention to them. All I could think about, all I could comprehend, was the beautiful wood and rust-free metal of the world's most magnificent sled. What did it say on the display at Skaggs? "THE MOST THRILLING WORDS IN ENGLISH: FLEXIBLE FLYER."

Indeed they were. And I was.

Thrilled.

"I wonder why Santa brought you a sled?" Dad asked, smiling broadly. "You already have a perfectly good one out in the garage!"

Dad's good-natured humor fell on deaf ears. This was not a time for banter or repartee. I grasped the edges of the sled firmly, squeezing the wood, running my fingers up and down the smooth surfaces. No splinters! No coarse wood! It was as slick as King Zor's plastic body, which now seemed to be chasing my hyperventilating sister around the room.

Carefully I lifted the sled to examine it more closely. It was heavier than I expected, and when I stood it up on end, it was almost as tall as I was.

"Wow," Max said. "That's a long sled." He turned to Dad, a little concerned. "Are sleds supposed to be that long?" he asked.

"As I understand it, they come in several lengths," Dad said, choosing his words carefully. "I'm assuming Santa knows that Sam is a good-sized boy and is going to get bigger. He needs a good, long, sturdy sled that's going to last him for a few years."

"I love it!" I said. "I'll bet a longer sled goes faster and turns better!"

I had no scientific basis for that assumption. But it sounded good.

"So Santa came up with a pretty good present for you, son?" Mom asked, her eyes shining with pleasure.

I looked at her. I couldn't find the words to express what I was feeling.

"He's real." That's all I could say as I pulled on the crossbar and watched how easily it shifted the shiny red runners one way and the other. "He's real."

Mom smiled, content at knowing that her baby was still a believer—for now, at least.

"That's good," she said. "Now, would you mind getting your dinosaur to leave your sister alone?"

Chapter Eight

For the next hour or so we unwrapped presents (I sat on the sled the whole time). Then Mom cooked a big breakfast of eggs, bacon, hash browns, and toast (I used the sled as a buffet table). Then we had the traditional Christmas fashion show, during which we tried on our new clothes, shoes, and galoshes (I used the sled as a runway). And then it was time—finally—to take the Flexible Flyer out for a ride.

"Let's take it to the same place we went yesterday," Dad suggested. "I'll bet we have a little better luck with this new sled."

So Dad and Max and I trudged up the hill in our new galoshes, which I thought were kind of cool because you could splash in huge puddles of icy water and not get your shoes wet—plus there was good tread on them to give you plenty of traction in the snow. Dad and Max took turns carrying the sled, and they talked about ways to attach a rope or something to the front so I could tow it rather than have to carry it. At the top of the hill behind the school, Dad put the sled on the snow and pointed it down the hill.

"Why don't I take the first run—just to be sure it's safe," he suggested.

"Actually," Max said, "I was thinking that maybe I should take the first run, since I'm smaller and lighter than you, and I'm not so . . . you know . . . fifty-two."

Max was clearly feeling the liberation that comes from knowing you're leaving home for two years (he was serving a mission like Mike had). Dad wasn't exactly sensitive about his age, but he was well aware that he was getting older, and he took advantage of every opportunity to prove that he still had the athleticism that made him a high school sports superstar back in . . . oh, let's see . . . 1928 or 1776 or 1492 or something . . . at American Fork High School, whose team mascot was—I'm not joking—the Cavemen.

"Doesn't anyone think that maybe I should take the first run, since it's . . . you know . . . my sled?" I asked.

"Well, you saw how it went yesterday," Dad said as he lay down on the sled. "I just want to make sure that you're going to be safe sledding here."

And with that, he pushed off, urging the Flexible Flyer down the steep hill—slowly at first, and then gathering speed as it cut through the snow with hand-crafted precision. By the time he got to the bottom of the hill, he was cruising at a pretty good clip, and you could probably hear his high-pitched "woo-hoo" in Salt Lake City.

"That was fun!" he shouted up from the bottom of the hill as he picked up the sled and started back up toward us. "It's a great sled!"

"Is it okay if I take the next turn?" Max asked me as Dad made his way to the top of the hill. "After that, it'll be all yours."

"Well . . . okay . . . I guess," I said, wondering if maybe the reason I got a big sled was that Santa knew mostly big people were going to ride it.

Dad handed the sled to Max, who took a few steps back and then ran forward with the sled, throwing it on the ground and then flopping on it while it was already starting to accelerate down the hill. Max was going even faster than Dad had gone, and the sled kept going for about twenty yards after it reached the bottom of the hill.

"Oh, so that's the trick—you get a running start," Dad said. "Do you mind if I try that really quick before you take over the sled?"

"Um . . . sure," I said. "That'll be okay . . ."

Max was flushed with exhilaration when he got back up to the top. "Bet you can't beat that record!" he said, grinning at Dad.

Dad took the sled from Max and walked back even farther than Max had.

"Bet I can!" he said as he ran toward the crest of the hill and vaulted himself and the Flexible Flyer down the hill. He was going faster than Max by a long shot, and he went farther, too— probably another ten yards farther.

"Oh, man," Max said. "He beat my record by a mile. I need to go one more time, okay? You don't mind, do you?"

Family pride and male ego were at stake here. At this point it really didn't matter whether I minded or not. Max was finally an adult and about to leave home, so he was physically challenging his father—testing his prowess against the alpha male; Dad, on the other hand, was not about to be defeated at *anything* by a young buck like Max, age fifty-two notwithstanding. These were not issues with which to trifle.

I stood at the top of the hill while Dad and Max competed in the first—and last—Andrews Family See How Far You Can Make the Flexible Flyer Go event. It was a loud and boisterous affair, consisting of multiple runs by each of the two adults (and I use that term loosely) present, ending with Dad holding the record (in no small part because he pushed Max off the sled as he launched his final attempt).

"Hey, Sam, is that you?"

Dad and Max were wrestling playfully on the snowy slope when Billy's familiar voice penetrated the Christmas air.

"Yeah, it's me!" I shouted to Billy, who was the first of a string of our friends pulling their sleds across the school playground and toward the hill. "That's my dad and brother. They're just . . . um . . . goofing around. They're not really . . . you know . . . fighting or anything."

At the time Dad was sitting on top of Max and was about to wash his face with fresh powder. Clearly, this was not the refined, dignified gentleman my friends were used to seeing, and they were a little startled. Dad rarely showed this side of himself around anyone except family. So he quickly stood, waved to the boys, and helped Max to stand.

"Well, it looks like your friends are here," Dad said as he brushed the snow off his jacket and pants. "Why don't you just stay and ride sleds with them, and Max and I will head on home?"

I was okay with that—especially since it meant I might finally get a chance to ride my new Flexible Flyer.

"Are you sure you don't mind?" I asked hopefully.

"Nah," Dad said. "Have fun. Mom said we'll have dinner in about an hour, so come home then, all right?"

"Okay," I said, although—let's be honest—I think we all knew that I had no sense at all for what an hour felt like, so Mom would probably end up sending Max back to get me. "I'll see you at dinner!"

"Hey, Sammy," Max hollered as he started back down the hill behind Dad, "Santa really came through for you! That's a great sled!"

"I know!" I shouted back to him. "It's the best . . ."

I didn't finish my sentence for two reasons. First, Max chose that exact moment to reach down, grab a big handful of snow and plop it on top of Dad's head before running full speed down the hill. Dad squealed like a little girl then took off after Max. I was intrigued by the match-up. Max was no doubt quicker at this point in their respective lives. But seriously, where was he going to go? He lived in the same house, for Pete's sake. Eventually he was going to be within arm's length, and Dad would get his revenge. Of that I had no doubt. Which is probably why my memory of the event includes a soundtrack—Sammy Davis Jr. singing, "What Kind of Fool Am I?"

The other reason I didn't finish my sentence is because just as Max was committing snowball patricide, Billy reached me at the hill's summit.

"Holy cow!" he said. "You really *did* get a Flexible Flyer!" Then he turned and shouted to the other guys still coming up the hill: "Hey, guys! Get up here! Sam got a new Flexible Flyer! And it's *huge!*"

Billy returned his attention to me and my sled. "I never saw a sled that long before," he said. "Are you sure it's a sled? Maybe it's a toboggan or something like that."

"It's a sled," I assured him as the other boys began to reach the top of the hill. "It's just big because I'm . . . you know . . ."

"Fat," Johnny said.

Jimmy dug an elbow into his brother. "He's not fat," Jimmy said. "He's just . . . big."

"But you said he was fat," Johnny said. "Then Mom said we shouldn't call him fat, so you said we should just call him—"

"Look at that sled!" Jimmy said, successfully diverting Johnny's attention. "Wow. It's long! How does it steer?"

"It steers great," I lied; I had no idea how it steered, because I had never been on it, except in the front room when I sat on it while we were opening presents. "Do you want to try it?"

"Sure!" Jimmy dropped his sled and was on mine faster than Bob Hayes in the hundred-yard dash. He pushed the sled about ten feet down the hill and then flopped on it and rode it to the bottom.

"That looked pretty fast," Billy said.

"But it's so long," Danny said. "It just . . . looks . . . funny . . ."

"Can I try it next?" Johnny wanted to know.

"Sure," I said. If nothing else, having the longest sled in the neighborhood would give me the novelty factor in establishing my position among my peers.

"Why don't you have a rope on this thing?" Jimmy asked when he finally got back to the top.

"We thought about that," I said. "We just . . ." I didn't want to admit that we didn't know where to attach it—especially since I could now see by looking at my friends' sleds what the hole on both ends of the handlebar were for. "We just didn't get around to it yet."

"Well, it's kinda awkward to carry up the hill," Jimmy said. "You really need a rope."

"My turn!" Johnny said as he grabbed the sled out of his brother's hands and took off down the hill.

"It's pretty fast," Jimmy admitted as he caught his breath at the top of the hill. "But it's kinda hard to turn."

"That's probably because it's so long," Danny said. "That's why it's so hard to turn."

"How do you know?" Jimmy asked. "You haven't ridden it yet."

"But I'm riding next, right, Sam?" Danny said.

"Sure—why not?"

Okay, I admit it—I was getting kind of mad. These guys were saying rude things about my new sled—my new, thrilling Flexible Flyer sled—which, by the way, they were all lining up to ride instead of their dumb little sleds of dubious ancestry. So what if it was longer than their sleds and a little harder to turn? What was wrong with being different? It was fast. It was fun. It was thrilling. And best of all, it was mine.

"Yeah, it is hard to turn," Johnny agreed. "I think there's something wrong with it."

"There's nothing wrong with it," I said. "It's a good sled. It's a great sled."

"But it's so long," Danny said. "That's what makes it so hard to turn. It's long."

"It's broke," Johnny insisted. "You got a bad sled."

"It's not broken, and it's not bad," I insisted, my anger beginning to show. "It's a great sled . . . the best sled up here!"

"Is not!" Danny said.

"Is too!" I replied.

"Is not!"

"Is too!"

"If it's such a great sled," Johnny interjected, "why are you riding it up here?"

I wasn't sure what Johnny was getting at.

"What do you mean?" I asked.

"Well," Johnny continued, looking at the other boys, "if I had the best sled in the neighborhood, I wouldn't ride it here. I'd take it to Mill Street and ride it all the way to Orchard Drive."

"Yeah," Jimmy said. "That's what you'd do if you had the best sled. You'd ride the best hill."

"Don't do it," Billy said. "If it's hard to turn, you'll never make it."

"That's right," Danny said smugly. "You'll never make it."

I should have hesitated. I should have thought it through—carefully. I should have considered all of the options and possibilities.

But I didn't.

"Yes, I will," I said. "I'll make it. You'll see."

The boys looked at each other for a moment. Then Jimmy smiled a knowing smile.

"Okay," he said. "Let's do it. Right now."

"Now?" I asked.

"Sure," he said. "Why not? It's Christmas Day. There's hardly anybody on the road right now, and there's fresh snow on the street. It's the perfect time to do it."

"Now?" I asked again.

"Yeah—now," Johnny said, picking up his sled. "Let's go."

"But . . . Danny wanted to ride the sled . . ." I said.

"It's okay," Danny said, smirking. "I'll ride it later—after you crash."

"Don't do it!' Billy said. "If you hit the curb hard enough, you'll ruin your new sled!"

Not to mention what it might do to me! I thought.

"But if you're afraid . . ." Jimmy suggested.

"Yeah. Nobody would blame you for being scared," Johnny continued.

"No one would call you chicken or anything," Danny added. Then he looked at Jimmy and Johnny and asked, "Would we?"

"No, we wouldn't," Jimmy said solemnly. The three boys looked at each other for a moment, straight-faced. And then they laughed.

"Okay, okay—we might tease you a little," Jimmy said. "But, honest, nobody will blame you if you don't do it."

"I wouldn't do it," Danny said. "Especially not on a big ol' sled that can't turn."

That did it. You can say I'm scared. You can say I'm afraid. You can even call me a chicken. But don't you dare call my beautiful new Flexible Flyer a . . . a . . . what Danny said.

Slowly I bent over and picked up my sled by one of its top rails. I looked at the boys' faces, then toward a long, steep street just a block or so away.

"Come on!" I said as I started walking down the hill. "Let's go take a ride on Mill Street!"

Chapter Nine

In real time, the walk from the top of the elementary school hill to Mill Street probably required only about seven minutes. But for a fourth-grader about to take his first-ever sled ride down the world's most perilous hill, it felt more like an odyssey of epic length—only without the nymphs and Cyclops and hydras and other cool stuff.

"Are you sure you want to do this?" Billy said as he and I walked together across the school playground. The other boys were dragging their sleds a few paces ahead, whispering and laughing and occasionally looking back at us.

"I'm pretty sure," I said. I nodded toward the boys ahead of us. "I don't think I really have a choice."

"Don't worry about them," Billy said. "None of them has

ever made it all the way to Orchard Drive, so it's not like they have anything to brag about."

I stopped in my tracks and looked at Billy. "They haven't?" I asked. "They all talk like they have."

"They're all big talkers," Billy said. "But as far as I know, my big brother Brent is the only one who has ever made it all the way, and he just made it last year."

"Then why are they so worked up about *me* doing it?" I wanted to know.

"Because you said you could," Billy said. "If you wouldn't have said you could do it, they wouldn't even expect you to try."

"Yeah, I know," I said.

We walked in silence for a couple of minutes while I considered my options. I could go through with it, which could result in my death or the destruction of my sled, which in turn would result in my death at the hands of my parents at home. Or, I could back away from my bold assertions and forever be known as a chicken and a chump, the kid who said he could— but wouldn't even try.

Which suddenly didn't sound like such a bad thing.

"Why are you guys going so slow?" Jimmy shouted back over his shoulder. "You're not going to ditch us, are you?"

I looked at Billy, and he looked at me. It wasn't a bad idea. If we ditched them, we would be guilty of a social faux pas, and we would take criticism for that. But I would still be alive, and my sled would still be in one piece. And no one would accuse us of being chickens—they would just say we were jerks.

I could live with that—*live* being the operative word.

But ditching the guys would just be putting off the inevitable. I knew that. At some point in time, I was going to have to either ride Mill Street—or not.

"What if you just tell them that you barely got this new sled and you need to ride it for a few days to kind of get the feel of it?" Billy suggested. "Anyone would understand that."

Billy had a point. Anyone *would* probably understand that. But the boys would remember. And so would I.

"I just want to get this over with," I told Billy. "I have to do this, so I might as well do it now and be done with it."

Billy nodded. He understood. So he walked with me toward Mill Street, like a priest walking to the execution chamber with a condemned prisoner, occasionally offering words of comfort and encouragement: "Nobody has ever died sledding Mill Street," he said. "Cameron's brother Brad had to go to the hospital for a week, but he didn't die."

Then later: "If it looks like you're going to crash into a truck, cover your face with your hands," he said. "It's better to get your hands cut off than your head."

I had pretty much resigned myself to pain and probable hand-lessness when we walked past the last house before the launch point at the crest of Mill Street. Suddenly a familiar and frightening voice penetrated the cold winter air.

"Mister Andrews!"

Only one voice could make my blood instantly turn to ice like that. Well, maybe two: Bette Davis and Clara Morgan. Not necessarily in that order. And since I was pretty sure Miss Davis wasn't spending the holiday on Mill Street, I assumed it was Mrs. Morgan who was calling to me. Then I looked and saw the horror in the eyes of my friends, and I was sure it was Clara.

I turned toward the sound of her voice, and there she was, her purple robe wrapped tightly around her, her head poking out between the doorway and the screen door, her bony finger beckoning me to come.

"Don't do it!" Billy whispered. "Christmas is the day when witches eat children!"

I have *no* idea where Billy got that piece of information. Probably the same place he learned that Ray Charles just pretended to be blind and that Ben Casey and Dr. Kildare were really brothers, or that John Wayne's real name was—are you ready for this?—Marion. He was always coming up with stuff like that.

Only this time I didn't buy it. For one thing, our family's pleasant Thanksgiving experience with Mrs. Morgan had pretty much convinced me that she wasn't really a witch. At least, not a full-fledged one. And even if she were, the thought of talking to her right now wasn't nearly as scary as the thought of lying down on my Flexible Flyer and sledding down Mill Street. So I walked over to her doorstep and followed her into her house.

"Would you like a piece of fudge?" she asked as she extended a plateful toward me.

"No, thanks," I said. I had never turned down an offer of fudge in my entire life, but my stomach was churning with pre-sled anxiety, and I didn't think it wise to eat anything at that moment.

She looked through her front window toward the boys who were huddled together at the top of Mill Street.

"Are you boys going to race down the hill?" she asked.

"No," I said. "Just me. I mean, I'm not racing or anything. But I'm going to ride down the hill, and they're going to . . . you know . . . watch."

She looked at me for a moment, then asked, "So you're the only one who is brave enough to do it?"

"Yeah," I said. "I mean . . . no . . . I mean . . . I don't know . . . maybe I'm the only one dumb enough to do it."

She laughed. "Well, you're not the only one," she said. "I've seen plenty of kids try it. I've watched them right here, from this window. Of course, I can't see them once they go past the bend in the road. But I've seen lots of them not make it that far."

"Did any of them . . . you know . . . die or anything?"

She laughed again. "No," she said. "Nobody has died. But a few of them got hurt a little. Especially that one boy who went right into the Kimball's pyracantha bushes."

"Yeah," I said nervously. "I heard about that."

"You could see the scratches on his face at church for weeks!" She laughed.

My stomach stopped churning. Now it was just hurting.

"You know," Mrs. Morgan continued, "I should probably call your parents and tell them what you're planning to do. They don't know about this, do they?"

"No."

"And I would call them too, if I thought you were in any danger. But if you'll do exactly what I tell you to do, you'll make it down to Orchard Drive without any problem. I promise."

I looked at her, trying to figure out if she had really said what I thought she'd said. Was this old, sick, frail woman really going to tell me how to safely ride my sled down Mill Street?

"Don't look so surprised!" she said, chuckling. "I've lived here for a long time. My boys were sledding that hill long before you were born."

"You have boys?" I asked. Somehow, it had never occurred to me that Clara Morgan was somebody's mother. She was just . . . you know . . . the old lady who chewed out the congregation at church. And maybe she was a witch. But a mother? No way!

"I have three of them!" she said. She walked over to her fireplace and took a framed photograph off the mantel, then brought it to show me. Three young men—probably about eighteen, fifteen, and twelve years old—smiled back at me. I had never seen them before, but there was enough of Clara in their faces that it was easy to believe that they were hers.

"They're all grown and married, and they have families of their own," she said. "They come here to see me as often as they can, but . . . they're so . . . busy . . ."

As an adult I might have noticed the sadness in her eyes and the wistful longing in her voice—especially on Christmas Day, which she seemed to be spending entirely alone. But as a nine-year-old boy, I just wanted to know one thing.

"So . . . they knew the secret to sledding down Mill Street?" I asked.

She smiled. "It's really not a secret," she said as she returned the picture to its prominent place on the mantel. "William—he's my oldest—he says it's simply a matter of physics."

"Physics?" That sounded suspiciously academic. Even though I didn't know what it meant, the word made me shiver.

"Physics is a kind of science," Clara explained. "It's about how and why things move. Every time my boys come back during the winter, they stand at this window and watch the sledders. And when someone crashes they laugh and say, 'They just don't understand the physics.'"

"But what . . . I mean, how . . . I mean . . ."

She smiled as I struggled to find the right words.

"You're not here for a science lesson, are you?" she asked. "You just want to know how to get to the bottom of Mill Street."

"Without crashing," I added.

"Of course," she said. "Without crashing. That goes without saying, doesn't it?

"Well, it's really simple, when you stop and think about it," she said. "All of the boys want to start on the right side of the road because . . . well, that's the normal side you drive on when you're driving on a road. They probably think it's safer to drive on the right side, and in a traffic sense, it probably is. But the first turn on the hill is a right-hand turn, and it comes right at the bottom of the steepest part of the street. So you're going pretty fast and trying to make a hard right turn, and centrifugal force—this where the physics comes in—pulls you to the left.

"Now, a lot of boys crash right there," she continued. "They can't hold that hard right turn when they're going so fast. And if they *do* make it through that turn by sliding to the left, they are now on the left side of the road going into the left-hand turn. So they're on the wrong side of the road for *that* turn, too. Instead of a wide, sweeping turn, they have to make another sharp turn, and that's where the rest of the boys usually crash. It's the physics, don't you see? They're fighting centrifugal force all the way down the hill, and most sleds aren't built to make those hard, sharp turns. But if they just start on the left side and then cross to the right side after the first curve, both turns are slow and gentle and easy, and you'll have no problem making it to the bottom."

She smiled triumphantly, as if she herself were now dancing in the middle of Orchard Drive at the end of a long, successful run. Then she looked into my glazed-over eyes and realized that the entire explanation had taken place about four feet over the top of my head.

"I'm sorry," she said. "Let me try to make it a little simpler."

"That would be good," I said. "I'm . . . you know . . . nine."

She took a deep breath. "Just start on the left-hand side of the street, Okaaay?" she said, a little *too* slowly. "Do you know which side is your left-hand side?"

"Yes," I said. "It's the other hand from the hand I write with. We covered that in kindergarten."

"Okay," she said. "Start your sled on the left-hand side of the hill."

"Left-hand side," I repeated. "Got it."

"You'll have to turn a little when the road turns, but that's all right," she said. "It's a much easier turn from the left side than it is from the right."

"Um, one thing," I said. "How exactly do I turn the sled?"

She looked at me suspiciously. "Have you ever ridden a sled before?"

I looked down at her brown-carpeted floor. "Well, once," I said. "Sort of."

"Those boys are trying to kill you," she said, a little angrily.

"Nah," I said. Then I thought about it. "Well, maybe . . ."

"Do you know that crossbar at the top of the sled?" she asked.

"The handle with the holes in it for your rope?"

"That's right," she said. "That's the crossbar. That's how you steer the sled. Just pull it toward you with your right hand when you want the sled to veer to the right, then pull it toward you with your left hand when you want your sled to veer to the left. Just remember, the sled doesn't turn like a car. It just veers a little—it doesn't turn completely. So if you want to change directions you have to give yourself plenty of time."

"Okay," I said. "I start on the left side of the road, and when I get to the turn I pull the steering thing toward me with my right hand to go to the right."

"Right!" she said. "That's it. Now, when the road straightens out there, keep going to the right, across the road. You want to be on the right side of the road for the next turn, which is to the left."

"That's a lot of rights and lefts," I said, still uncertain I understood completely.

"Let me try it this way," she said. "For the first turn you want to be on the left side of the road. After the turn move across the road so you're on the right side for the second turn. Does that make sense?"

"Start on the left," I said. "First turn, be on the left. Second turn, be on the right."

"That's it!" Clara seemed pleased. "That's all it takes! See, it really is simple!"

It really was. It was so simple, I figured there had to be a catch.

"What happens after that?" I asked.

"After the second turn, you need to start dragging your feet so you can stop the sled before you get to Orchard Drive," she said. "This is very important. You've got to promise me you'll stop the sled before you get to Orchard Drive. That's a busy street. You don't want to ride the sled out into the middle of it. Okay?"

"Okay," I said.

"Do you promise?"

"I promise!"

She looked at me and smiled. "Then I think you're ready!"

We walked toward the door, and she rested her hand on my shoulder, giving me a quick little hug as I went outside.

"Thanks, Mrs. Morgan," I said as I picked up my sled. "I'll let you know how it goes."

"Oh, don't worry about that," she said. Then she pointed toward her window. "I'll be watching!"

Slowly I walked out toward where the boys were gathered in a small, frightened circle at the top of Mill Street.

"Where have you been?" Billy asked.

"I was just talking to Mrs. Morgan," I said.

"We thought maybe she ate you," Johnny said.

"Yeah," Jimmy said, "and we were afraid she was going to come for us next."

"I don't think she's really a witch," I said. "She's really pretty nice when you get to know her."

"She cast a spell on him," Danny said to the other boys. "That's why he thinks she's nice. She cast a spell on him, and now he's a walking zombie."

"Yeah, I'm a zombie," I said as I walked toward the left side of the road. "And I'm going to be the first zombie to ride Mill Street all the way to Orchard Drive."

I put my sled down on the crest of the hill and prepared to board it.

"What are you doing?" Jimmy asked.

"I'm getting ready to . . . you know . . . take off," I said.

He shook his head. "You can't start from over there," he said. "It's dangerous."

"Why?" I asked.

Jimmy looked at the other boys for help. But they didn't have an answer, either.

"Well, that's just how it's done," Jimmy said. "You always start on the right side."

"Well, maybe that's how you guys do it," I said as I knelt beside my sled. "But I'm trying to look at this scientifically, and centerfield force tells me I should start on the left."

"Centerfield force?" Billy asked. "What's that?"

"It's physical," I said smugly. "You know—science. It just means I should start on the left."

"Man, you're going to do one of those 'agony of defeat' things on *Wide World of Sports*," Danny said. "You'll see."

"Maybe I will," I said. I put one knee up on my Flexible Flyer and prepared to push off. But before I did, I glanced up at Mrs. Morgan's window. She was there—watching. She waved and smiled. I smiled right back. Then I lay down on my belly on top of the sled, grabbing the crossbar firmly with both hands and bracing myself for what would either be the greatest moment of my young life—or the worst.

I was surprised at how quickly the sled gathered momentum as I started sliding down the left side of Mill Street. The cold breeze bit into my chubby red cheeks, and I squinted my eyes against the flecks of ice and snow that were blowing into my face. I could hear the whoosh of the sled's bright-red runners sliding smoothly over the snow and ice as we raced down the hill and toward the first turn. I pulled down on the crossbar with my right hand. Mrs. Morgan was right—it didn't turn like a bike or a car. I was heading directly toward the curb on the left side of the street, so I pulled harder on the crossbar. Gradually, the sled started to veer to the right—not sharply, but enough that I avoided crashing into the curb.

By now I was past the steepest part of the hill and still moving down Mill Street at a pretty good clip. The wind whistled in my ears as I continued to urge the sled toward the right side of the road. I wanted to look back to see if the boys were still watching me, but I didn't dare take my eyes off the road ahead of me—not to mention the Kimball's pyracantha bushes on the right side of the road were approaching a little too rapidly for my taste. I straightened my grip on the crossbar, and the Flexible Flyer obediently straightened its path down the hill. When the road started to veer to left I veered along with it from my place on the right side of the road. It was smooth and gentle and easy—just as Mrs. Morgan had said.

I was just coming out of the second turn and heading into the last, long, straight stretch to Orchard Drive when I noticed the familiar gold Impala coming around the corner and heading up Mill Street. Thankfully, the Impala was on my left, so we could pass without getting in each other's way (although the car did splash a little slush on me as I flew past it). I wanted to wave at whoever was driving Dad's car, but I didn't dare take my hands off the crossbar. Besides, there was something else I was supposed to do. Something important. Something I promised Mrs. Morgan that I would do before I got to . . .

Orchard Drive! It was looming large in front of me, and I could see the cars whizzing through the intersection in both directions. I tried to dig my galoshes-covered toes into the snow, but I was going so fast my feet kept bouncing off the icy track. I was just a few houses from the intersection and preparing to roll off my new Flexible Flyer, sending it on down the street to certain destruction on Orchard Drive, when the snow surface beneath me turned slushy and the sled slowed noticeably. The closer I got to the intersection, the slushier the surface became. Finally I could drag my feet, and I brought the sled to a stop a few feet before the stop sign on the corner of Orchard Drive and Mill Street.

I lay there for a moment on my sled. My mind raced to comprehend what had just happened. It was over. I had actually done it. I had ridden my new Flexible Flyer sled all the way from the top of Mill Street to Orchard Drive. None of my friends had ever done it. But now I had. And I wasn't exactly sure what to do next.

The honking of a car horn behind me suggested in a not-so-gentle way that perhaps the thing I ought to do next was get out of the street. I rolled off the sled and picked it up and carried it to the sidewalk. That's when I noticed that the car behind me was the Impala, and the driver was my brother Max, who jumped out of the car and ran over toward me. At first I thought he was going to share in the exhilaration of my moment of triumph.

Instead, he brought me firmly back to earth.

"What are you doing riding your sled on the street like that?" Max demanded. "I almost ran you over back there! And who knows what would have happened if you had slid all the way out onto Orchard Drive!"

"I was okay," I said. "I made it all the way from the top of Mill Street—"

"Does Dad know you were going to sled on this street?" he asked.

"Um, I think I mentioned it to him once . . ."

"Well, he's going to be mad when I tell him about this," Max said. "And I hate to think what Mom will do."

"But I was the first—"

"Put your sled in the backseat," Max barked as he walked back to the driver's side of the car. "Mom sent me to get you. You're already late for dinner."

And just like that, the thrill of victory became . . . well, you know . . . less thrilling.

I put the sled on the backseat and closed the door just as my friends came running around Mill Street's second bend, waving and hollering wildly. I waved back and smiled bravely. Then I turned to get in the car and head home with Max to eat Christmas dinner—and to face the parental music—with the quiet dignity befitting the kid who had conquered Mill Street on his Flexible Flyer sled.

Epilogue

Mrs. Morgan was right. It really was all about the science.

Not just the ride down Mill Street. But all the stuff that happened afterward, too. It was all just reaction in response to action.

Like my conversation with Max on the way home to Christmas dinner. When I explained to him why I was sledding on Mill Street, how it was all about trying to fit in and to find my place among my new circle of friends, he understood. He told me about how hard it had been for him to leave Arizona and all his friends right after graduating from high school, and how hard he had worked to fit in with the boys in Utah. For him, it didn't happen on Mill Street but on our driveway basketball court. But he understood the need to fit in. And somehow in the moments we sat together in the Impala, talking before we went into the house, a few barriers melted away and we became closer as brothers, bound by newfound commonality.

"So where did you find him?" Mom asked as we walked in the back door together.

"He was just sledding," Max said. "I guess he lost track of the time."

Mom smiled as she poured raisin sauce over the holiday ham.

"Well, maybe he'd do better if he had his own watch," she said.

"I know I would. I'd never be late again if I had my own watch."

"Well, why don't you go look in your stocking?" Mom smiled. "I don't think you looked very carefully in there. You might find something interesting."

Mom was right, of course. In all the excitement of King Zor and the Flexible Flyer and everything, I hadn't really looked in my Christmas stocking. So I went out to the front room and dumped it out. Sure enough, there was a brand-new Timex ("takes a licking and keeps on ticking!") in there, just my size.

Now, I'm not saying I got a new watch for Christmas because I made it all the way to the bottom of Mill Street on my new Flexible Flyer sled. I'm just saying it was a great Christmas—maybe the best ever—and all of this great stuff was tied together somehow. Scientifically.

Like in physics, you know?

Which reminded me . . .

"Hey, Mom," I asked as I ran back into the kitchen, "do we have enough food for dinner?"

She looked at me, wondering if perhaps my new watch had cut off the circulation to my brain. "When have we ever *not* had enough food?" she asked.

"Well, I was just wondering if maybe we had . . . you know . . . some extra food today."

"There will be plenty of dinner, I assure you," she said. "Why?"

"I don't know," I said. "I was just . . . sort of . . . wondering if maybe . . . you know . . . it might be a good thing to invite Mrs. Morgan to have dinner with us."

"I'm sure she's with one of her boys today," Dad said.

"No, she isn't," I said. "I was just up there. She's alone today. And . . . well . . . it wasn't so bad having her on Thanksgiving, so maybe . . ."

"I thought you said she was a witch!" Linda said.

"Nah," I said. "There's no such thing as witches—especially on Christmas."

"Well, I think that's a great idea!" Mom said. "Let me call to invite her." She glanced at Dad. "I'm not making any gravy today, so I think we should be safe."

And that's how Clara Morgan came to spend Thanksgiving *and* Christmas with us. And it's why she and I spent a good deal of time during Christmas dinner giving each other knowing winks and smiles.

Then there was the thing with Ann—that was *definitely* an equal and opposite reaction. It came at the end of dinner, after the last crescent roll had been eaten and the last bite of bread pudding had been consumed. Mom suggested that Linda and I do the dishes. And I was okay with that. Linda had her own way of doing the dishes, which meant that I just needed to stay out of her way until she was ready for me to dry. So I went out to the front room to play "King Zor Flattens Barbie and Ken"—much to Ann's consternation. When Linda called to let me know she was ready for me to dry, I turned off King Zor and got up to go into the kitchen.

That's when it hit me.

"Hey, just a second," I said to Ann. "I got a Flexible Flyer sled for Christmas, didn't I?"

"Yes," Ann said as she tried to reaccessorize Barbie and Ken after the most recent dinosaur attack.

"And didn't we have an agreement about what would happen if I got a new Flexible Flyer sled for Christmas?"

Ann stopped. "An agreement?" she asked. The scrunched-up look on her face suggested that she couldn't quite put her finger on it.

"Dishes," I said. "You get to do my dishes."

"Oh, that's right," she said, clearly not happy about it. "I do your dishes for a week."

"Uh, no," I said. "For two months."

"Two months! I'm sure I didn't agree to that!"

"Actually," I said, "it was your idea."

"I think that's wrong," she said. "I'm going to tell Mom."

"Good idea," I said. "Tell Mom that you were betting me on whether or not there is a Santa Claus. She'll like that."

I had her, and she knew it.

"Two months," she muttered as she trudged into the kitchen to begin paying off her bet. "This doesn't mean there's a Santa Claus, you know!"

Actually, I thought it was pretty good evidence that there *was* because I was getting everything I wanted for Christmas—including retribution.

In a scientifically reactive sort of a way.

The day after Christmas I met my friends on top of Mill Street, where I explained to them the science of successful sledding. They all followed my instructions, and they all made it successfully to Orchard Drive—several times, in fact—without so much as a close call with the Kimball's pyracanthas. The ride down Mill Street became so common and ordinary that we went out in search of something more exciting. And when we went searching, I was one of the guys. I wasn't the new kid, or the big kid, or the kid who has never been on a sled before. I was the kid who flew down Mill Street.

Which wasn't quite as heroic as President Kennedy staring down Castro and Kruschev during the Cuban Missile Crisis. But for a nine-year-old trying to fit in with his new neighbors, it was close enough.